FRONTIER WALTZ

"You stay away from me, mister, or you'll be sorry," the diminutive brunette cried out at her grinning adversary.

"Have you never been to a charm school, Miss Madeline?" Cain King asked, mocking her.

"Listen, White Bear, I mean it!" Madeline warned.

"Call me Mr. King, if you please," King said softly, then lunged at her, quick as a cat. She managed to dodge to the left, then darted to the abandoned pool table, grabbed up a cue stick, and swung it at the advancing giant.

He didn't duck quite fast enough and the butt of the cue caught him a glancing blow close to the top of his white head, but in a moment he had her wrapped up close to him, helpless in his big arms.

The cue stick fell to the floor as she went limp.

"Darn you, King," she said weakly, a hint of the come-hither in her voice now that she was safely trapped.

"May I have this waltz, Miss Madeline?" King smiled down into her dark features. "Maestro—" King spoke to genial Herman Stock. "A waltz, please."

PRAISE FOR JACK CURTIS'S PREVIOUS SAM BENBOW WESTERN

BLOOD TO BURN

"Jack Curtis's . . . latest Pocket Books Western . . . *Blood to Burn*, [is] worth every penny."
—Eli Setencich, *The Fresno Bee*

W9-AVY-034

PRAISE FOR OTHER JACK CURTIS WESTERNS

PARADISE VALLEY

"Memorable images sparkle through this 'flight-delay Western.'"

—Books of the Southwest

THE JURY ON SMOKY HILL

"*The Jury on Smoky Hill* is the best Jack Curtis book so far, with plenty of mystery and suspense."

—Wayne Barton, coauthor of Manhunt and Live by the Gun

"Once again Jack Curtis brings us a novel of the Old West that has a storyline that is as old as the West but as refreshing and new as the spring air and flowers of April and May. Curtis makes it easy for us to lean back and relax and enjoy an hour or so away from our daily cares. We are treated to an exciting, suspenseful drama. Run, don't walk, to the nearest bookstore and purchase this book."

—Don Warren, The Western Review

BLOOD CUT

"This is a book for all 'old west' fans. The author takes you back in time to when men were men and you knew who the good guys were. He also makes you feel that you are there as he characterizes his characters in such a believable manner. This is the best new Western novel that I have read in some time. Make this a must on your list."

—Don Warren, The Western Review

MORE PRAISE FOR JACK CURTIS

TEXAS RULES

"The conclusion, which I will not give away, furnishes an original twist for what is in the first two-thirds of the novel a fairly traditional story fraught with a love interest, villains, and, as expected, a stampede. In *Texas Rules,* Curtis has produced a good powder-burner that will leave readers satisfied that western writers, though using a familiar form, still possess the ability to provide a new wrinkle for an old story."

—Lawrence Clayton, *Abilene Reporter-News*

"A smoothly written adventure . . ."

—*Books of the Southwest*

"Curtis pushes all the right buttons in this novel just as he did in *Blood Cut.* . . . This book is even better than *Blood Cut* and I thought that it was the best new Western novel that I have read in a long time. Buy it and read it. Cotton Dunbar is a strong character and if John Wayne were alive and this was made into a movie he would be ideal for the role. . . . A dynamic, action-packed novel . . ."

—Don Warren, *The Western Review*

THE SHERIFF KILL

"Fine Western adventure featuring a complex antagonist. Heartily recommended."

—*Booklist*

Books by Jack Curtis

The Mark of Cain*
Cut and Branded*
Wild River Massacre*
The Fight for San Bernardo*
Blood to Burn*
Paradise Valley*
The Jury on Smoky Hill*
Blood Cut*
Texas Rules*
The Sheriff Kill*
Red Knife Valley
Eagles Over Big Sur
Banjo
Klootchman

*Published by POCKET BOOKS

Most Pocket Books are available at special quantity discounts for bulk purchases for sales promotions, premiums or fund raising. Special books or book excerpts can also be created to fit specific needs.

For details write the office of the Vice President of Special Markets, Pocket Books, 1230 Avenue of the Americas, New York, New York 10020.

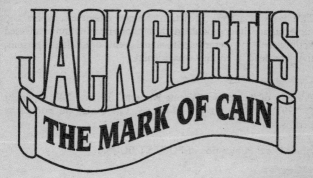

JACK CURTIS

THE MARK OF CAIN

POCKET BOOKS

New York   London   Toronto   Sydney   Tokyo   Singapore

The sale of this book without its cover is unauthorized. If you purchased
this book without a cover, you should be aware that it was reported to
the publisher as "unsold and destroyed." Neither the author nor the
publisher has received payment for the sale of this "stripped book."

This book is a work of fiction. Names, characters, places and
incidents are either products of the author's imagination or are used
fictitiously. Any resemblance to actual events or locales or persons,
living or dead, is entirely coincidental.

Portions of the article "Writing Westerns" by Jim Cole, copyright
© 1991 by *Coast Weekly*, Monterey, California, are printed by
permission.

An *Original* Publication of POCKET BOOKS

POCKET BOOKS, a division of Simon & Schuster Inc.
1230 Avenue of the Americas, New York, NY 10020

Copyright © 1994 by the Curtis Family Trust

All rights reserved, including the right to reproduce
this book or portions thereof in any form whatsoever.
For information address Pocket Books, 1230 Avenue
of the Americas, New York, NY 10020

ISBN: 0-671-79316-0

First Pocket Books printing January 1994

10 9 8 7 6 5 4 3 2 1

POCKET and colophon are registered trademarks of
Simon & Schuster Inc.

Cover art by Lino Saffioti

Printed in the U.S.A.

THE MARK OF CAIN

— 1 —

THE RIDER, NONDESCRIPT EXCEPT FOR A FADED BLUE FROCK coat, a looped-up kossuth hat revealing shaggy red hair, and brass gooseneck spurs left over from the war, came up the trail alone. His horse was a copper-bottom stud, and his stock saddle had been made in Mexico.

One man, alone in the enormous Montana country, became faceless, nameless, as insignificant as an afterthought of the gods, and this rider rode with a sense of humility that the grandeur imposed upon him.

The trail he'd taken east from Virginia City was not overly used and was sometimes covered by tall bluestem grass, which also hid the bones of buffalo that had been slaughtered to force the Sioux and Blackfeet on to the north.

He wasn't worried about getting lost. He could see the line of alders and cottonwoods along the river, and on upriver he knew he would find Elk City. Far off in the distance he could make out a range of snow-covered peaks, and overhead the sky seemed bigger than any in Texas because it was a paler, cleaner blue.

The ball containing 550 grains of lead that smacked

1

him high up between his broad shoulders drove him clear of his stirrups and over the stud's head before the report of the .45 caliber Sharps rifle reached his lifeless body, which still twitched spasmodically in the crushed and bloody grass.

The spooked stud ran, and a long silence hung over the land as the bushwhacker waited to make sure his shot was true. Over the fine rolling country, even the meadowlarks and red-winged blackbirds ceased to sing, and a vulture appeared as an idly circling speck in the pure blue sky.

A strong pale gray gelding carrying a heavily built man, with his long-barreled rifle cradled over the pommel of his saddle, and leading a white pack mule, emerged from a coulee to the northwest and approached the fallen rider at a slow trot. Coming close, the big man dismounted awkwardly because of a shortened and sprung right leg, crabbed forward warily, and laid the muzzle of the Sharps on the red hair spilling down over the dead man's neck.

The bushwhacker shook his blocky head in disappointment, then rolled the rider over with his boot.

Staring down into the open, opaque eyes, he clamped his lips tightly together in exasperation and said, "Who the hell are you?"

Rare here on the northern prairie, his drawl carried a certain southern gumbo richness.

Taking a printed poster from his inside coat pocket, he studied the sketch and read the description once again.

"Y'all got the frock coat, got the hat, got the right build, but you surely are not Red Handley," he grumbled. "Wasted my cartridge on you."

Not being a thief, he left the body and limped back to his horse, his huge torso bobbing and swinging like a rocking chair with each step.

Dressed in greasy, smoke-tanned buckskins, heavily armed, and well mounted, he rode away down the trail.

His short, prematurely white beard and long hair did little to soften either the flinty angles of his face or the dissatisfaction on his twisted mouth.

His name was Cain King. Sometimes he was called the White Bear, and sometimes he was called the King of Death.

=== 2 ===

ONCE THE BLACKFEET WERE MOVED OFF TO THEIR RESERVA-
tion and Texas cattle were coming in to replace the
buffalo, Elk City was ready for the boom. Already it
boasted a general mercantile, barbershop, harness mak-
er, blacksmith, carpenter, land office, doctor's and lawyer's offices, a bank, livery barn, three saloons, a new
brick jail, and the marshal's office.

It was in that short ticktock time in western America
when one great historical people was all but extin-
guished, its vast herds of buffalo slaughtered close to
extinction, leaving the bone-rich ground to a new race
with its own vast herds ready to move in.

And Elk City, situated at the junction of Bridger's Fork
and the Elk River—once a fur trappers' rendezvous—
was a product of that historical moment and the biogra-
phy of the big, empty country.

It could be reached by stage or small steamer, but the
railroad was yet to come, and early on, the city fathers—
that is, the banker, the merchant, and the lawyer—
fearing their isolated vulnerability, hired an aging gun-

fighter as marshal and built him the single-cell jail with the office in front.

The old gunfighter served well enough in his rough, hard-drinking, poker-playing fashion, but last March when the snow was thinking about melting, he was caught drunk and in a cross fire at the same time, leaving the city fathers to seek out another peacemaker.

Young Marshal Sam Benbow, sitting at the battered rolltop desk, was trying to open up a package of Wanted posters tied with twine that had just arrived on the noon stage.

It being Monday, the jail was empty and the town tiredly tranquil after its usual weekend hoo-raw.

A lanky, rusty-haired six-footer with a long face and mule-shoe jaw, showing the weather marks of having lived in the saddle most of his nearly thirty years, he little resembled the bloated gunfighter he'd replaced last May.

His big fingers, callused and rope-burned, fumbled with the knots on the package. He knew he could get out his jackknife and cut the twine easily enough, but he had a conservative nature, and preferred to save the binding for another day.

For him the posters were a waste of time anyway unless one of the wanted men happened to blunder into town and started a fuss.

The descriptions were too general, and the portraits fuzzy and out-of-date. It was just more government foolery.

Sure, if an ornery cuss came into town, pulled his six-gun and shot up the street, then yelled he was Buzzsaw Brown from Cow Creek, Kansas, likely that would fit a frazzle-bearded, one-eyed mug on a poster, but things like that just never happened.

Still, it was part of his job to post them up on the soft pine bulletin board. Five days a week you did this fiddle work, and on Saturdays and Sundays, you threw the crankiest drunks into the cell to chill off, then Monday morning bright and early, you kicked them out whether they felt like travelin' or not.

Once in a while a new herd would come through from Texas with a bunch of thirsty drovers and you'd have to settle 'em down some. But if you talked slow and simple, recalling your own younger days, families, cousins, and old-timers in Coleman County, pretty soon you'd meet some shirttail kin, and the word would get around that the marshal was not only big and salty, he was a Benbow from Texas.

Aside from keeping the cowboys from goin' crazy, there wasn't much else to bother. There was talk of some young misfits, eastern gutter rats, clewing up in the badlands, but so far it was just a lot of smoke and no fire.

Sooner I get shut of this job and get back to settin' a horse, the better, Sam thought, feeling a sudden longing to be out on the open range.

Soon as Buddy shows up, we're dustin' out of here, he promised himself. Then he wondered why he had to keep making excuses for taking the fool job and holding it for the past month.

He and Skofer Haavik—the older rapscallion who had ridden with Sam in the cavalry—had come drifting through, looking for a special lay of land where they could bury their tormented pasts and start all over again.

Sam had returned from the hard-fought, tragic war to northern Colorado to confirm that the Arapahoe girl he'd married before the war started and their child had been killed in an unprovoked massacre by the Colorado Volunteers. He'd gotten word of it just before the Battle of Lookout Mountain, but had steadfastly refused to believe that western settlers could be so savagely merciless until he'd returned to find the Valley of Many Mink empty of people.

Distraught by the loss of his beloved, his soul burned

and mutilated by the hideous war, he'd roamed back down to Texas, drinking, quarreling, fighting, killing, until he'd come across old Skofer in El Paso in about the same condition.

A fearless fighter in Stuart's Cavalry brigade, Skofer had also been its chaplain because he'd been a professor of theology at the University of Virginia before joining up.

After the surrender, he'd returned to Charlottesville to find that he had nothing left, no family, no property, not even his faith. Good-naturedly he'd refused to face the facts of life by going on a binge of forgetfulness that carried him farther and farther from home.

When they met again, as they had in the army, each started looking out for the other, sympathizing with the other's problems while ignoring his own, each trying to mend the other's mangled spirit while forgetting his own irreparable losses.

With Sam's brother Buddy and a homeless crew, they'd mavericked a herd of longhorns around the home ranch and headed north in two sections, Buddy's outfit trailing behind.

They'd hardly unpacked their saddlebags before the Elk City fathers had sized Sam up and said they'd find him the right ranch if he'd be patient and act as marshal till they could find somebody else.

They hardly counted Skofer in because he looked like a scruffy rat terrier, short of teeth, rheumy-eyed, and as gun-shy as a female institute. Neither Sam nor Skofer bothered to correct their judgment. Skofer looked as poor as a desert grasshopper, but he made a lot of whoop and holler.

Now a month had gone by and neither Elam Castor, the banker, nor the mercantile owner, Max Zink, had turned up anything suitable.

There was still the Bohannon Bench to look at upriver,

but he thought it better to wait for brother Bud to sell his half of the herd to the miners in Virginia City, and come along.

As soon as Bud caught up with them, they could ride up near the Blackfeet feeling fairly sure they'd get back alive.

Meanwhile, he was drawing down thirty dollars a month and his room in the back, which was some better 'n nothin'.

Dang it, he thought, why am I settin' here, all thumbs with a bunch of paper pictures, when I could be out yonder on the grassland?

"Care for a fresh chocolate-filled doughnut, Marshal?"

The young, teasing voice of Sally McKenzie broke into his musings and he looked up to see a small, dark-haired lady—lady or girl? He couldn't decide.

She was at least eighteen, but she had such a confident, carefree manner, she seemed more like twelve. With round, merry, freckled face, dark hair touched with reddish highlights, and a quick, agile way of moving, she had become a pest to him in some ways, always bothering him to try some new fancy pastry that he had no taste for.

"Thanks, I'll pass, Sally," he said politely, not looking up from the hard knots that eluded his blunt fingers.

"I made them myself from an old army cookbook recipe." She smiled.

"I was a Reb," Sam said.

"All corn pone and blackstrap molasses," she teased. "What have you got against the finer things in life?"

"Them things always have to be paid for sooner or later," he said heavily.

"One way or another." She mimicked his slow, deliberate speech, and he looked up at her, annoyed.

"Okay!" she giggled. "I'll be going now, Mr. Sam. Don't bother to try holding me against my will!"

Dang females, he thought, they don't have any respect

for a man anymore. A man says something serious, they mock him.

Then he thought, Sam, you are gettin' to be a little stodgy in your old age, and smiled at himself.

He knew little about her except that her father was a career soldier, and with nothing else to do, she'd come to help old Ira Armsbury out at the café. An ex-cavalryman, Ira had lost a leg fighting the Cheyennes, and somehow she knew him and his wife, Ada. That was about it.

From outside on the boardwalk, Sam heard the high banshee voice, accompanied by the keening howl of a tone-deaf dog, wailing:

> "O the minstrels sing of an English king
> Many long years ago . . ."

"Damn it, Skofe," Sam yelled, "have you picked up another stray mutt?"

> "Who ruled his land with an iron hand
> Although his morals were weak and low. . . ."

The duet of howling, yipping, yowling, bawling, and caterwauling voices continued without a pause.

> "He loved to hunt the royal stag
> That lived in the royal wood,
> But better than that he loved
> To stand as the royal stud. . . ."

Sam looked out at the gnomelike Skofer waving both hands at the sitting airedale, conducting *con gusto,* his bloodshot eyes on those of the long-nosed dog.

"Skofer, it's too early for music lessons . . ." Sam muttered, "and too early to be drinkin', too. . . ."

Without glancing up or losing a beat, Skofer led the intent airedale on to the chorus:

"All wild and woolly and full of fleas,
His terrible tool hung down to his knees,
God save the barsted King of England. . . ."

"Skofer, cut out the damn chin music and get in here,"
Sam yelled.

"Old Barney, he's a very quick learner. I will teach him
La Nozze di Figaro next," Skofer murmured happily,
coming inside and looking at Sam with owly eyes.

"You been drinkin'," Sam said, not accusing but with a
certain exasperation in his voice.

"Just one little drink to tune my vocal chords," Skofer
chuckled, then paused and frowned. "I'm supposed to
tell you Pat Duveen wants to see you."

"Someday you'll make sense in one word or less
maybe," Sam grumbled. "Now, can you just tell me just
what the hell you mean?"

"Calm down, Captain." Skofer smiled, delighted that
he'd cracked the granite calm of his young partner. "It's
just they's a couple youngsters on the prod."

"They lickered up already?"

"They're workin' at it with new money." Skofer nodded, licking his lips. "I thought I'd go back and help 'em
out."

"You open these up, sort 'em out, pin 'em up." Sam
put the package in Skofer's hands. "I need a recess."

"I saw 'em first!" Skofer protested.

"But I'm boss." Sam smiled faintly. "Just open up the
cell door and keep out of the way."

Quickly striding out the door, big-shouldered Sam
crossed the street to the Bonny Kate Saloon, paused a
moment at the batwing doors, then pushed through and
quietly strolled over to the long bar as if he hadn't a care
in the world.

Right off he noticed the two young dudes, but he kept
his gaze on Pat Duveen, the portly bartender.

"A beer, Pat."

The bartender drew a glass of beer, set it on the bar in front of Sam, then wiped his pink hands on the towel around his ample waist.

"Kind of quiet today," Sam murmured.

"Mondays generally are." Duveen nodded, his eyes flicking off toward the pair at the end of the bar.

Turning and noticing the old Regulator clock on the wall behind them, Sam murmured idly, "Funny nobody ever shot the clock."

"They know better," Duveen said. "I brought that clock all the way up from St. Louis."

They were a pair, all right. One was thin and pasty-faced, with little pig eyes; the other was dark and looked like a catfish with a wispy mustache. Both wore two six-guns, slung low, and both had quit talking.

The pasty-faced one stared at Sam, and after sizing him up, made a sneering smile, pointed his forefinger at the clock, sighted over it, and said, "Bang! Bang! Dead clock."

"Good shot," Sam said.

"Bull's-eye. Lonnie never misses," the other said loudly.

"What do you do in this burg besides take care of the clocks?" Pasty-faced Lonnie's laugh was more like a silly giggle.

"We whittle some," Sam said, hoping a little joke would cool them down.

"We don't like whittlin'," Lonnie snarled suddenly. "We like a lot of thunder and lightnin', don't we, Frank?"

"Give us another shot of that panther piss," catfish Frank said, tossing a shiny new gold piece on the bar.

Duveen waddled over and refilled their shot glasses.

"Where's the women?" Lonnie demanded.

"Mondays they generally take a rest," Duveen said. "Come back tomorrow night, boys."

"Good Christ, what kind of a town is this anyways!" Frank downed his drink. "We got money and we want to burn it!"

"And we don't care what day it is or what your damned clock says." Lonnie spoke softly, but his eyes were afire.

"Likely they's a squaw down at the Topaz. That's just down the street," Duveen said quickly.

"We heard there was a real beauty here with an ass like a guitar," Lonnie said.

"That'd be Madeline," Sam said. "She's restin' upstairs."

"Well, are you goin' to go bring her down, Marshal, or do I got to do it myself?" Lonnie demanded, a little smile playing on his full lips.

"Neither, I reckon," Sam said. "Mondays we just set."

"What the hell you talkin' about?" Frank pawed at the air as if it were thick with smoke.

"Best haul your ashes down to the Topaz." Sam nodded.

"Like hell!" Lonnie's eyes gleamed wickedly.

"Stayin' long?"

"We ain't stayin'. We just come in, and after a while we're just leavin'," Frank said quickly.

"Where you boys from?" Sam asked.

"Downriver." Lonnie smiled.

Sam looked them over and failed to match them up with the variety of Wanted posters he'd looked at. They were too young to be that important. Either that or the federal marshal's office was about ten years behind in their posters.

"And I suppose you're goin' upriver?" Sam responded casually.

"That's right," Frank said.

"Not much back up there. Peters out into badlands. Lookin' for work?"

"We're lookin' for fun, Marshal." Lonnie giggled

12

sharply again, his eyes going wild. "Wake up them whore gals!"

"You know it's my job to corral the different kinds of hardcases that come through," Sam said conversationally. "You might say after a while a man gets to be pretty fair at readin' the brands on different types of critters."

"You callin' us critters?" Lonnie slowly turned so as to face Sam directly.

"I'm talkin' about my job. If I wanted to shoot you, I'da already done it," Sam said, keeping his voice tuned slow and easy while his deep-set eyes concentrated on the pair's every move. "I'm beginnin' to wonder why youngsters like you are drifting along upriver."

The swarthy one, without a signal, sidled away from the bar, a move that would put Sam in a cross fire.

"Hold it there, boy," Sam said. "You take another step and I'll drop you. Get on back to the bar, so I can talk to your sidekick."

They were as deadly as small rattlesnakes with new poison, Sam thought as he waited for Frank to make his play.

"We didn't come in here for shootin', Marshal," Lonnie said, taking the edge off his voice.

"I see the hardcases, I see the fool kids who don't know better 'n to tie their trigger back," Sam said, "but you don't fit either way."

"It's a small town," Lonnie said.

"And it's my town." Sam smiled, flicking his eyes to Pat Duveen standing bowed over with his hands hidden behind the bar. "Show 'em the greener, Pat."

Pat, no longer the jolly fat man, brought up the sawed-off two-bore and thumbed the rabbit-eared hammers back to full cock.

The pendulum on the old Regulator clock on the wall marked the silent seconds with a loud and relentless ticktock, ticktock, taking the time away and putting none back.

"Now, then . . . left-handed, shuck the gun belts, boys," Sam said.

"What the hell did we do?" gritted Lonnie as his partner started to comply.

"I told you. Mondays is a quiet day in Elk City, and you wasn't payin' attention."

"I don't give a dog fart about Elk City any day of the week!" Lonnie took half a step away from the bar, his hands hovering over the walnut grips of his six-guns. "How about just you and me makin' a play. Leave them two out of it."

"Not a chance." Sam smiled, shifting his weight, then abruptly leaping off his cocked right leg, his rock-hard fist coming across and catching Lonnie under the jawbone.

The young gunman dropped like a sack of oats, his eyes rolling upward.

As Sam unbuckled Lonnie's gun belt, he remembered how Marshal Bill Tilghman lost his life to an overlooked hideout pistol, and patted down the groggy Lonnie. A long, thin knife was hidden in one boot, and a pouch of new gold pieces in the other.

Frank, the dark one, had a derringer instead of a knife in his boot, but his leather pouch of gold pieces was identical.

"Help your sidekick across the street to the jail," Sam said. "I want to study you over some."

"We ain't done nothin'!" Frank said.

"What you did was wool me wrong," Sam said. "Get your butt movin'."

As Frank looped his arm around Lonnie's shoulder, Lonnie's eyes opened and he glared up at Sam. "Damn you to hell, Marshal, you can't hold us!"

"We'll see," Sam said mildly. "Now, let's take a *pasear* yonder where you can rest on a bunk instead of the floor."

=== 3 ===

Sᴀᴍ Bᴇɴʙᴏᴡ ꜱᴛᴏᴏᴅ ᴀᴛ ʜɪꜱ ᴅᴇꜱᴋ ᴀɴᴅ ꜰʟɪᴘᴘᴇᴅ ᴀ ꜱʜɪɴʏ twenty-dollar gold piece spinning into the air and caught it in his left hand.

"How come them brats each got five hundred in new gold?" he asked Skofer, who occupied a wired-together hickory chair near the door.

"Maybe they come from a rich family." Skofer shrugged his thin shoulders.

Sam set his jaw tight as an iron wedge. "Not likely. Cutthroat river rats is what they look like to me."

"After we've turned 'em loose, there'll be some Wanted posters come on the next stage sayin' they're worth a thousand dollars dead or alive," Skofer said, and stood up to look out the door.

"You want to go beat on 'em with a single-tree?" Sam asked, shaking his head with disgust.

"I reckon you'd have to burn their feet off before they'd answer up," Skofer said, looking up the street, then added, "Oh, Lordy . . . here comes the White Bear."

Cain King, on his pale horse and leading a buckskin

and a packed white mule, rode down the street from the west. Draped over the buckskin's saddle and tied neatly was a dead man in a blue frock coat.

"Who is it this time, King?" Sam asked as the big, white-haired man dismounted in front of the office.

"Name's Red Handley. Wanted for murderin' a lawman in San Antonio." King brought out the Wanted poster and handed it over to Sam.

"See? He's got the birthmark on his neck and lost his left thumb."

"And redheaded." Sam nodded. "Mind takin' him around to the back door of the barbershop before a bunch of kids show up?"

"It won't hurt 'em to see death in all its glory."

"Skofe," Sam said, and Skofer stepped forward, took the lead rope, and led the buckskin with its grisly burden down the alley before the town folks had time to congregate.

"How'd you take him?" Sam asked grimly, already aware that Red Handley had been shot through the shoulder blades, the bullet going on through into the heart.

"I can kill a bug on a flea's belly button at five hundred yards." The big man smiled thinly.

"Suppose it wasn't him, though?"

"It was him. Just fill out the paper and give me a chit on the bank," King said, then added, "if you please, sir," as if remembering his southern manners.

Sam went back into the office and found the proper form to certify that Red Handley had been brought in dead and that Cain King was authorized to take the reward payment of one hundred dollars.

To Sam it was a sickening business. Certainly the country would be better off without the Red Handleys, but it seemed like there ought to be a better way to get rid of them.

For that matter, why didn't they put a bounty on corrupt politicians?

Sam Benbow wished he was a hundred miles from this office where he had to do too many things that went against the grain of a common cowpuncher lookin' for a home.

"I'll go with you," Sam said, handing the signed form over to the bounty hunter, whose buckskins gave off an aroma stronger than campfire smoke.

"That might save some time," King said, his voice deep and rich as Mississippi mud. "Mr. Castor always seems to think he deserves a percentage of my reward."

Sam looked at Cain King carefully. He'd been acquainted with a few southern gentlemen in the war, and he knew a lot of roughneck cowboys, army people, nesters, and ordinary business people, but he'd never known a man who could speak in such different voices, who lived off blood money like a savage, yet could sometimes stand tall and make a commanding figure in spite of his foul buckskins.

Who was this slovenly giant? Where did he come from? How had his leg been maimed? Why did he live to kill?

What curse lay behind those clear azure eyes that seemed to burn like the blue opals of hell?

"You always ride alone?" Sam asked.

"Always. Ever since the war."

"Deep South?"

"My home was in Mississippi," King replied, "and my hair was black."

"You're still young enough to start over," Sam persisted.

"It isn't always age that turns a man's hair white." King nodded, then his manner changed and his voice came out harshly. "What the hell are you waitin' for? I want my money and I want my woman!"

17

"Wearin' a badge makes a man nosy," Sam said.

They walked to the corner where the new two-story bank building stood, mounted the steps, and went inside.

The dimly lit room smelled of the oiled pine floor, dust, and money. There was no one behind the teller's cage, and they continued on to the back of the long room and found the frog-breasted banker standing in his office doorway.

Short and pudgy, he held himself erect, but still failed to make his chest bigger than his belly, and the smile on his pale, porky face reminded Sam of a gila monster observing a nest of baby mice.

"I'm sorry, but we're closed," the banker said. "My teller has gone home."

"I want my money," King said, tossing the authorization on the desk. "I don't care if you're open or closed."

"If you want special service, you'll have to pay for it."

"You get your end from the government," Sam said. "You can't charge twice."

The banker fixed his small, reddish eyes on Sam and shook his head. "There is a ten percent charge for this sort of transaction."

Suddenly King drew a gleaming bowie knife from his upper boot, and drove it through the authorization deep into the oak desktop.

"I want my hundred dollars, right now." His whisper held more menace than the roar of a grizzly sow with cubs.

"I'll see what I can do." Castor smiled rigidly, took five gold pieces from his vest, and handed them over to the big, white-haired man. "Anytime I can help, just let me know."

King said nothing as he jerked the knife free and stabbed it back into its scabbard. Glaring wildly at Castor and then Sam, he turned and limped heavily back out the door.

"That man's insane!" the pudgy banker said weakly. "He ought to be locked up."

"Can't lock him up for askin' what's due him."

"He threatened me with the knife. You saw that!"

"You tried to euchre him out of his reward." Sam shrugged. "I've got to get back to the jail. Got a couple of young river rats to look after."

"River rats?" The banker's eyes flickered. "What have they done?"

"I don't know, but I mean to find out," Sam said over his shoulder as he went out the door.

Once outside, he realized he'd felt so anxious to get away from the oppressive atmosphere in the bank, he'd forgotten to ask if there was any news about a ranch for sale.

From the Bonny Kate Saloon across the street he heard a yell and the sound of breaking glass. Drawing his Peacemaker, he ran across the street and through the batwing doors.

Pat Duveen was climbing to his feet from behind the bar, his face pale as whey cheese.

"What's the trouble?" Sam asked, looking about the room littered with broken glass.

"The White Bear is the trouble," Duveen said, pouring himself a straight shot of red whiskey. "I told him the girls took Mondays off."

"Shouldn't have done that." Sam had to work to keep from smiling. "Where is he?"

"Upstairs." Duveen jerked his head toward the stairs. "You'll hear her scream in a minute. He's an animal!"

"I've got to watch the jail," Sam said, trying not to hurry out the door.

As Sam came inside the office, he shook his head and muttered, "I've about had enough."

"I don't blame you much." Skofer laughed at Sam's stubborn features, which were now overcome by bewilderment and disgust. "That Cain King, he'd spook a dead cow in a mudhole."

"I thought it'd be a quiet Monday." Sam smiled ruefully. "Now I'm worryin' about Tuesday."

"I spoke some with that Lonnie boy, but he don't say much except a few things reflecting on my sainted mother."

Sam hung his hat on a nail and went down the hall to the barred cell door.

"You boys 'bout ready to give me some identification?"

"My name's Lonnie Sackbutt," the pasty-faced youth snarled. "He's Frank Arbole. That's all there is."

"Where you from?"

"I told you. St. Louis."

"And you're just goin' upriver to look at the Indians."

"I'm hungry," Frank Arbole said.

"There'll be some beans for supper likely, and breakfast, too."

"We haven't broke any laws anywhere," Lonnie Sackbutt snarled. "You got no right holdin' us!"

"You keep sayin' the same things. Why don't you tell me about your folks, where they are, how long you been gone? Does your ma miss you? Who do you work for? Things like that."

"It ain't none of your business," Frank Arbole retorted. "Can't you get that through your hammerhead? It just ain't none of your business unless we commit a crime."

"Where'd the thousand dollars in gold come from?" Sam asked idly.

"We found it downriver." Lonnie grinned, showing his rotting teeth.

"Layin' on the trail, I suppose."

"We come on the steamer," Frank Arbole said. "We found it layin' there on the deck."

"In two separate bags, just like that?" Sam murmured.

"That's right. Finders keepers," Lonnie said.

"Maybe I'll just keep it here until somebody claims it," Sam said. "You wouldn't mind that, would you?"

Before either of the young gunmen could answer, a voice from behind Sam said, "I would mind that a great deal, Marshal. I must say I mind this whole foolhardy proceeding."

Sam turned to see a slim, dark man with flourishing black sideburns, with a silver-handled cane hung over his left wrist.

"You're the lawyer?" Sam asked.

"Yes. Randolph Jack. I've just recently hung up my shingle upstairs over the bank."

"I always heard if there was just one lawyer in a town, he'd starve to death," Sam said.

"Ah, you have a sense of humor, Marshal," Randolph Jack said without smiling. "Now, please release these innocent travelers and I'll be on my way."

"What's your interest in this?"

"It is my profession to uphold justice."

"I don't want a lot of cool blue smoke, I just want to know who hired you."

"That, sir, is private and privileged information, which I cannot divulge. Suffice it to say, I see two innocent boys locked up in this foul prison by your whim and am determined that they be released this instant."

"Or?" Sam asked blandly.

"Or I'll have you up before the judge for kidnapping and malfeasance of office."

"I guess the judge won't be by for another couple of weeks," Sam said laconically.

"For every day you keep these boys locked up without justifiable charges, I will ask the judge to fine you one thousand dollars. You will not trifle with liberty, Marshal, not while Randolph Jack is still able to breathe!"

Sam wasn't so much worried about the lawyer's threats as he was about just what was his duty. He had no legal training, and only a smattering of book learning, but he'd passed the bar of experience with hardened fighting men in the most adverse of conditions, and he trusted that experience most times.

But now he was caught between what he knew in his heart and what was the extent of the marshal's duties. His job was to keep the peace in Elk City. Nothing had been said about general outlawry outside in the new territory. In practice either the U.S. Marshals handled it, or, if it got far out of hand, the vigilantes would take over.

As he considered the question back and forth, Elam Castor came in the front door, looked at Skofer at the desk, then down the hall at Sam and the lawyer.

"What's going on here?" he demanded, advancing on Sam with his back straight and his chest up.

"We're discussin' liberty and justice," Sam said, frowning.

"Not quite. The marshal here is detaining these innocent boys without any charges," Jack interjected.

"That's not a good way to encourage folks to come to Elk City," Castor said. "I'm sure Mr. Zink and Mr. Starbuck will agree."

Sure, Sam thought, they all owe you money.

"You found me a ranch yet?" he asked suddenly.

"No—not yet. I have several good prospects, though," the banker replied. "Now, what about these prisoners?"

"I promised I'd take this job if you found me a little ranch I liked, but you don't seem to be lookin' too hard."

"Let's keep to the subject at hand," the lawyer said, stroking his curly sideburns with a pink finger.

"It's true I can't charge 'em with anything illegal," Sam said, disgusted with his job and himself. "I'll turn 'em out, but they're leavin' town and no mistake about that."

Sam glared at the banker and the lawyer, as if daring them to object, but they both smiled like jackasses eating cactus. Sam nodded to Skofer and turned away.

As Skofer hunted for the key, Sam went across the street to the Bonny Kate and settled himself at the end of the bar.

"Glass of beer," he said grumpily, sending the signal that he didn't need companionship.

Him and Skofer'd come up over a month ago, knowing nothing of the country except what old Buck Bohannon had told them about the spread the Blackfeet had chased him off of.

From what the old man had said, Sam thought he could make a go of the ranch as the Blackfeet slowly pulled back north, but he had never got past this ratty town.

Darn it, he thought, why didn't we just keep goin'?

Then he remembered the first day in town when he was buying supplies for the trip to Bohannon's Bench, and the lady in Zink's Mercantile had smiled at him when he asked for a box of salt herring.

"It's a weakness of mine, like sorghum is for others," he'd explained, embarrassed and stammering. Then he realized he was staring into her blue eyes and watching her pretty mouth and the way her yellow hair swished back and forth around her long, fine features, and when she asked him where he was staying, he had no answer.

"I don't know. . . ." he'd stammered, not able to say he meant to keep on travelin' and would sleep on the ground that night.

"Ma Riordan has rooms," she said. "I'm staying there with my father until school starts, then I'll be teaching." Her accent was eastern, and she spoke with quiet dignity.

"You don't work here permanent?" he'd asked, feeling a sense of confidence with her, the same as with his sisters.

"No, I'm green as grass." She had smiled. "My home was in Washington, D.C., and my name is Jean Louise Starbuck."

Then she'd started talking softer and more thoughtful, in a way no one else could, open and friendly like, and next day they offered him the marshal's job.

=== 4 ===

THE SUN WAS SETTING TOWARD THE WEST WHEN SAM stepped out of the Bonny Kate. He was feeling better, more sure of himself now that he'd thought things over and made his own independent plans.

Not completely independent. Skofer had to be considered, and he needed to talk some with Jean Louise before he could go roaring off upriver.

But as he strolled down the boardwalk, he understood that he was wasting his own good time waiting for Buddy and playing the puppet for Elam Castor and the rest of the businessmen in town.

Turning in at the double door of the mercantile, he saw old Zink at the side counter, and smelled the new leather of factory-made shoes, the soaps and colognes, dried apples and dried currants, the piney scent of green lumber, and the rich smokehouse flavor of sausages and hams hanging from a ceiling joist in back.

Off to the left he saw Jean Louise measuring out a length of Turkey red calico for a lady.

Stopping at the counter where the grizzled old German cut wedges out of a wheel of yellow cheese with a long butcher knife, Sam nodded and said, "Town's quiet now."

"Ja, it's better to get rid of those rubbish kids." Zink looked up at Sam. "I hope they go clear to the Blackfeet and get their tongues cut out."

"If I'da had a couple days with them, I might have found out what sort of deviltry they were up to."

"Better they go and leave us be." Zink grunted. "We want a quiet town."

"I reckon it's steadied down enough so I can take a pasear up towards Bohannon's Bench."

"You said you'd stay here and be, Marshal. You don't get paid to ride all over the country," Zink said, not looking up from the cheese wheel.

"Nobody has found anything for me."

"It takes time."

"Fix me up a pack of provisions, half a side of bacon, cornmeal, cheese, biscuit, some dried apples, and salt herring."

"We want you in town in case there's some other kind of trouble, like from that crazy bounty hunter," Zink said quickly.

Two ladies with children came in the front door and made their way over to the dry goods department, where Jean Louise was just finishing wrapping up the calico yardage.

Sam mentally kicked himself for having held back to talk to the German. Now he'd never get a chance to speak to her alone.

She looked at him across the counters piled with a variety of goods, smiled, and shrugged her shoulders.

Sam thought he'd never seen anyone so ladylike and fine.

Turning back to Zink, Sam said evenly, "Skofer can handle the job until Saturday. If you've got something as good as Bohannon's and closer to town, I might change my mind."

"Let me talk to Mr. Castor," Zink said worriedly. "You never know what's in his head."

Sam wished Buddy would hurry. The ranch wasn't just his idea, it was all of them together, and he didn't like making decisions that might not be agreeable later on.

Besides, a month of spring was already gone, and though winter looked a long way off, it really wasn't when you measured the time in fixing up an abandoned ranch, laying in firewood, feed, and stocking cattle.

As another lady with two young boys entered and headed for the dry goods section, Sam gave up hoping they would all leave and let him have a free minute with Jean Louise.

Tipping his hat to her, he walked on out to the street. He'd try to see her later on at the rooming house and tell her his plans.

Looking up and down the nearly deserted street slowly falling under the yellow dusk, he wondered for a moment if maybe he wasn't taking too much for granted. After all, she was devoted to her dad, who seemed to have a lot of problems, and he didn't want her to get the wrong idea about his intentions.

Turning right, he walked the half block to the corner where the small livery barn was situated. It was a hurry-up building, the green lumber already warping and shrinking, but inside, the smell of sweet grass and the pungent, honest smell of horses lifted his heart. In the corridor between the banked stalls, he found old Milt Koberman dumping oats from a quart measure into the feed boxes, already polished by horses' nibbling muzzles.

"Howdy, Sam." The old man squinted up at him with cloudy eyes that were losing the battle with cataracts. It was a question, Sam thought, of whether the old man would die or go blind first, either one being a final curtain for a man who had sided Jim Bridger early on.

"How's my Big Red?" Sam asked.

"Needs work."

"I'll take him out in the mornin' for a few days. I want to look at the Bohannon place."

"That's upriver." The old man nodded.

"You know it?"

"Spent time there, yes, before Bohannon."

"He said it was a punch bowl with plenty of grass in the bottomland."

"It is." Milt Koberman nodded. "Only one way into it is through the gap in the rimrock, and if the river floods the gap, then there's no way out except through the Blackfeet reservation."

"He said he'd built a cabin and sheds and such."

"Too close to the Blackfeet. They the meanest redskins I ever seen."

"I hear they're tamin' down some with the TB and the smallpox."

"They wasn't no ways tame whenever I tangled with 'em." Old Milt Koberman shook his head.

"But you still have your hair." Sam smiled.

"Only because I wanted it more than they did!" The old man cackled and sighed, remembering.

Sam leaned over the plank barrier and patted the big sorrel's neck. "Ready to run, boy?"

"He's shod well, but barn-sour. Likely he'll knock the gate down goin' out." Old Milt grinned.

Saying good night, Sam walked out into the twilight, crossed over, and ambled up the street to the jail, where Skofer was just lighting a coal oil lamp.

"I'm thinkin' of ridin' up to the Bohannon place in the mornin'," Sam said.

"I don't like the tone of your voice, Captain," Skofer said. "Sounds like I'm goin' to be left home to tend the nursery."

"Somethin' like that." Sam nodded. "We promised 'em law and order, and if we both go, it wouldn't do."

"Besides, you been gettin' nervous as a chippy in church anyways."

28

"I was hopin' I could send you and Buddy on up ahead, but it ain't workin' out that way."

"He'll be along about any day now."

"But the days keep goin' by, and we're not movin' with 'em. I sure don't want to winter here."

A scream ripped through the dusky street, and Sam whirled to pinpoint its source before it sank away.

"The Bonny Kate . . ." he muttered, and ran across the street at a diagonal, with Skofer right behind him.

Slamming through the batwing doors, Sam saw a small woman with an hourglass figure moving around a poker table as Cain King circled along after her. Her hair was blue-black and her skin dark, in sharp contrast to the whiteness of the bounty hunter's, and her low-cut purple gown came from a world different from that of his grimy buckskins.

Sam looked questioningly over the heads of the by-standers at Pat Duveen and saw Pat shake his head, as if to say, *No, leave them be.*

In the group itself were old Doc Newlin, Will Reese, the barber and mortician, Randolph Jack, a couple of cowboys, Herman Stock (with his accordian draped over his chest), and Dixie, a jolly, fat, baby-faced sporting girl enjoying the scene.

"Hit him again, Madeline!" Dixie yelled. "Give him a good one, right on the button!"

"You stay away from me, mister, or you'll be sorry," the diminutive brunette cried out at her grinning adversary.

"Have you never been to a charm school, Miss Madeline?" King asked, mocking her.

"Listen, White Bear, I mean it!" Madeline warned.

"Call me Mr. King, if you please," King said softly, then lunged at her, quick as a cat.

She managed to dodge to the left, then darted to the abandoned pool table, grabbed up a cue stick, and swung it at the advancing giant.

He didn't duck quite fast enough, and the butt of the cue caught him a glancing blow close to the top of his white head, but in a moment he had her wrapped up close to him, helpless in his big arms.

The cue stick fell to the floor as she went limp.

"Darn you, King," she said weakly, a hint of the come-hither in her voice now that she was safely trapped.

"May I have this waltz, Miss Madeline?" King smiled down into her dark features.

"You're so rough," she protested in a small voice.

"Maestro . . ." King spoke to genial Herman Stock. "A waltz, please."

Herman Stock stretched out the accordian as he remembered a melody, then squeezed it, bringing out the first swinging phrases of "The Blue Danube."

The crowd moved aside as King released the small Madeline and bowed elaborately.

"May I have this dance?"

"Well, sure, Mr. King, if you want," Madeline replied.

Taking her by the hand, and holding her at a proper distance, King swung her into the waltz, and despite his maimed leg, was able to bob and weave and make the swirling circles creditably, his back straight, his head high, a smile on his face, and a distant look in his eye, as if he might be back in Mississippi, perhaps on the plantation at a summer party with the girl of his dreams.

Sam, along with the other onlookers, stood frozen in wonder at the transformation of the pair. King dancing in the celestial spheres, Madeline, her eyes closed and her pouting mouth parted in a rare smile, changing the raw saloon into an elegant ballroom with a special magic.

As the waltz drew to a close, King held Madeline's left hand with his own, bowed, and said, "Thank you, dear lady. Shall we retire to the veranda?"

"Gosh, Mr. King, I dunno. . . ." Madeline started to object again, but without waiting, King lifted her in his arms and started carrying her up the stairs.

"Now that we've graduated from charm school, my dear, it is time you went to finishing school." He smiled at her.

Sam wasn't sure if it was a joke or not. He was sure, though, that the King of Death was short a few pieces of furniture in his upstairs parlor.

Sam wondered at that. How dangerous is a man so big and powerful, a man deadly with the long rifle, who spends most of his time in a world all his own?

He was heading for the door when Elam Castor entered, his chest perked up and his head as tall as he could stretch his neck.

"Ah, Sam . . . Marshal Benbow, I'm glad to see you. We have good news!"

Sam felt like looking for a hole to hide in as he looked into the glittering gila monster eyes.

"What would that be?" he asked neutrally.

"Let me buy you a drink, Marshal." Castor took Sam by the elbow and guided him to the bar. "What'll you have?"

"Glass of beer," Sam said to Pat Duveen.

"The same." The banker smiled and turned to Sam. "Have you ever heard of the old Coyote McSwayne ranch down on Yellow Creek?"

"Can't say as I have." Sam shook his head.

"It's back up against the Absarokas. Pretty place. McSwayne brought in some railroad Irish to build his spread, but the Sioux sluiced the whole bunch before they ever finished. The ground is proved up, and McSwayne's widow has authorized me to sell it for whatever I can get."

"Sounds promisin'," Sam said, wondering why the opportunity popped up just as he was set to ride the other way.

"I've drawn a map of the trails and streams. You go take a look at it and we'll talk some business," the banker said genially.

31

"I don't want to waste my time on a wild-goose chase, Mr. Castor," Sam said levelly.

"It's up to you. There's three sections, three square miles leapfrogging down the prettiest little stream so as the whole shebang is all yours for the taking."

"I'd kind of set my sights on the Bohannon place upriver."

"Dangerous up there," the banker said. "Renegades, road agents, outlaws, riffraff . . . and the Blackfeet besides."

"Sounds like they need a lawman more 'n Elk City." Sam smiled, testing the banker.

"It's too soon." The banker's face darkened. "Another ten years, maybe those folks up there will get themselves sorted out."

Sam looked at the map the banker had drawn and said, "How will I know I'm at the right place?"

"You'll find log buildings still standing. You'll find a graveyard where they were buried, and you'll see McSwayne's brand burned into a board on a wagon wheel as you're going in."

"What was his brand?"

"The Irish cross." The banker dipped his finger into his beer and then traced the symbol on the bar: ✝

"Looks more like a double cross to me."

"It's not important, just look around and we'll go from there."

"All right, Mr. Castor, I'll take a look." Sam glanced at the old Regulator clock on the wall, and shook his head. "Gettin' late, and I've still got things to do."

Touching his hat, he hurried out to the boardwalk and, seeing the mercantile was dark, walked down the side street to Ma Riordan's rooming house, hoping he could talk to Jean Louise before she went to bed.

He didn't know exactly what he wanted to say, but somehow he felt it was important to just tell her he was going off for a couple of days so that she wouldn't worry.

They'd never talked much. He'd never said anything about the future except what he was looking for, and she hadn't led him on any whenever he talked about that.

There was still a lamp lit in the dining room when he went up the steps of the big, boxy house that had been added on to several times since mountain man Jim Bridger had rendezvoused near here in a tepee forty years before.

At the dining table, Jean Louise sat reading a book by the light of a large hanging Rochester lamp.

Hearing his footsteps, she looked up and asked, "Dad?"

"Sam," he said, coming into the light.

She rose and took his hand for a moment, looking up into his eyes questioningly.

It wasn't that she was so small, it was that he was just a lot bigger than she, he realized. She was dressed in a white blouse and gray skirt, her yellow hair braided up into a crown on the top of her head.

"How are you, Sam?" she asked. "Please, sit down." He took off his hat and sat in a straight-back chair like a proper schoolboy waiting for instruction. "Relax a little, Sam." She smiled. "How was your day?"

"Normal."

"The man called the King of Death brought in a body?"

"Bounty."

"Have you heard from your brother?"

"No, ma'am."

It was no wonder she thought that the Texas cowboys, who were normally so afraid of women and ordinary society, would go completely crazy once they were away from home and loosened up with liquor.

"Have you heard anything of a ranch hereabouts?"

"Banker Castor, he thinks there's a half-finished spread off west a ways and some north that might do."

Gradually he explained the few details he knew of the history and location of the spread, when she thought, Why am I doing this? Why am I talking to this good cowboy as if I could be friendly with him, as if I were leading him on?

"Somethin' wrong, ma'am?"

"Please call me Jean, Sam." She tried to put on a smile.

"What's wrong? I say somethin'?"

"No, Sam. It's not you or your fault. It's something I can't talk about."

"I figure we're friends," Sam said.

"Ah . . ." She sighed and looked away. "That's my problem. I wish it could be more, but I have my father to look after. I can't leave him alone."

"I can understand that," Sam said stolidly, unaware of the desire that shone in her eyes.

Sam already knew the old man spent most of his time hanging around the Topaz, a dingy sort of knocked-together saloon where the rotgut was cheap but still overpriced.

"He's trying to write the history of western politics," she said. "He thinks he has to mingle with all sorts of people to be able to get a clear picture."

"I thought he was a politician of some kind," Sam said, wondering why she'd quit looking him in the eye.

"He writes articles for the eastern periodicals." She worried that Sam would think she was a brazen hussy for being so forward.

"I admire anybody that has an education. If I could write, I could sure tell some stories."

"Sam," she said seriously, "listen to me. I don't want you to get the wrong idea, and I don't want you to be hurt by expecting something from me I can't give."

"I'm not expecting nothin', Jean Louise," Sam said softly.

"Just so you know," she said, with a hint of moisture in her eyes. "My duty is to take care of Father. I have been doing it for some time, and I will continue."

"Sure," Sam said. "We all look after our parents. Me 'n Buddy looked after Ma as long as she lived."

"I'm glad you understand."

"But I reckon I can get along with your dad all right, even if he's an educated, highfalutin history writer." Sam smiled, trying to lighten up her mood.

"It's not—" She never finished the sentence, as she heard a thumping noise at the front steps and a small, groaning curse.

"That'll be him," she said quickly, and hurried out onto the front porch.

Edward Starbuck was gripping the stairway railing with one hand, trying to lift himself up off his knees.

"Dim dammit," he muttered, as Jean Louise took him by the shoulder and got him to his feet. "Dad-rat it, girl, leave me be!"

Shaking free of her, he struggled up the steps to the porch, where Sam stood in the lamplight of the open door.

"Whothehellareyou, mister, and whatareyoudoing with my daughter?" Mr. Edward Starbuck snarled, his words coming out slurred and angry, whiskey talk.

"This is Sam Benbow," Jean Louise said in a weak voice. "He's the town marshal."

"I know. I know. You don't have to tell me," the older man in his dusty suit and crooked cravat mumbled. "But we have broken no statutes and soon enough we'll have the whole pie, and we don't need you around, Marshal, to cut it up with."

"Dad!" she exclaimed, shocked at his rudeness.

"It's all right, Jean Louise. Sometimes the educated ones tear loose just like a Texas cowboy, only they do it some different," Sam said patiently. "Want me to help you put him to bed?"

"Nobody's putting me to bed, Mr. Marshal, whoever the hell you are, messing around with my daughter! Out!" The irate and intoxicated author lurched on through the door.

Jean Louise looked at Sam with imploring eyes and said, "I'm sorry, Sam."

"I'll see you when I get back."

He pressed her hand gently, then turned and went off into the darkness.

=== 5 ===

DAYBREAK FOUND SAM ON THE TRAIL WESTWARD, WHICH would lead eventually to Cooke City in Wyoming Territory, unless he took the north fork—as he intended— which would end up in Virginia City. He had no intention of going that far. The map indicated he'd follow the trail westward some thirty miles, then hook off to the north a mile or so up Yellow Creek to the McSwayne ranch.

It was the same trail Buddy should be following over from Virginia City, and Sam was hoping they might meet up on the way.

Once he was clear of Elk City, Sam's heart lifted. When Big Red was warmed up, Sam let him loose in a long lope, until he felt the big horse slow and his breath rattle, then he reined him back down to a steady, easy trot so he could get his wind and settle himself into the long trip.

"Feel good being loose?" Sam said to the powerful horse, who still thought he ought to be running full out. Still Sam held him back. He knew where they were going, and the horse didn't.

Going downriver, Sam felt the power of the new country, the richness of the deep grass, yet the emptiness of it all. Someday it might be full of people and cattle or sheep or something worse, but now it was as the Indian had left it. Deer, elk, antelope, were too small in the measure of the curved earth to even count. What had counted was the great, almost limitless herds of buffalo. They had made a dent in the landscape, but the hide hunters had simply killed them all. They'd set up the Sharps on a rest and just knock the buffalo down one at a time from a distance, bushwhacking them so they never knew what was killing them, never could make a defensive ring of bulls around the cows and calves because the rifle was completely out of their blood knowledge, and they would have needed at least a thousand years to develop a defense against it. More unprepared for guns than the Stone Age Indians, the buffalo never knew what happened to them. They stood milling about, pawing the prairie, looking about with nearsighted eyes, bellowing, and dying.

The meat was left to rot. Years later the bones were gathered up in wagons and sent east on railway cars to fertilize that tired soil.

The tall, gray-green trees along the river sparkled with the morning dew, and the clear, splashing water sent mirror flashes through the dappled tree trunks. He could hear the thunking of water dropping into deep pools and the roar of the white water when the rock bottom turned or narrowed into a torrent.

The river was big enough to accommodate small steamers, but only in the spring and early summer. Later on, after snowmelt had ended, it would lower into a tangle of huge boulders and old snags that made navigation impossible.

It was nothing to Sam. He believed only in the horse as a way of transportation. As a toddler, he'd napped on the belly of a great mare in foal, and he'd been lifted into a slick fork Texas saddle when he was three or four. It seemed like he'd never gotten off.

Growing up, he'd watched to make sure the mares ate the slick membrane off from the newborn foals so that they might breathe, and he'd watched the old, ringboned ones decide it was too painful to get up in a frosty morning, and shot them cleanly between the eyes. He'd ridden the feisty ones, the lazy ones, the good ones, and the fiery ones, and understood them all.

He classed Red as a fiery horse who would never be content to slog along. He was a horse who would have been fine in battle before guns were invented. Before you ever thought to say giddap or squeeze your knees or lean forward, he was already going.

But then, horses weren't everything in the world. Maybe they were important to him, but Sam wondered if the historical writer Edward Starbuck ever had been astride one. Probably he hired a hack or rode the stage if he was traveling anywhere, and cared nothing about the animal that moved him from one place to another.

Sam realized his own limitations. The horse was half his own life, but not necessarily anything in other folks' lives. Maybe someday the horse would go the way of the buffalo. Folks would ride the steam trains or boats or on each other's backs, and the horse would be sold for his hide.

It seemed that just as one valley pinched out, another greensward would open up, with the river meandering over from one side to the other, bounded by the rising hills that would end in jagged peaks too steep for anything except for a few marmots, mountain sheep, and eagles.

There were no settlements along the trail, only an occasional stage stop, few and far between. The ranches were generally set off on their own, not bothered by every passing rider or stagecoach, but the way stops were a part of the trail and provided hard bunks, country cooking, and some care for your horse.

Generally they were run by women who'd outlasted their men, because a woman knew how to serve and take care of people, whereas a man chased steers and broke horses, both hazardous pursuits.

True enough, his woman was generally overworked and might wear out from childbearing every year, but there were always a couple, three, old-maid aunts or sisters about to help split the wood and milk the cow, grind the mush and sweep the floors.

These thoughts floated idly through Sam's mind as he traveled the long way westerly with only the long grass and an occasional badger or coyote to talk to besides Red.

He smiled as he remembered a yarn about John Purdy and his wife standing at the way station waiting for the stage, and his neighbor comes along and says, "Goin' on a pleasure trip, John?" "Nope," John says, "the wife's goin' along."

What had Jean Louise meant when she said she didn't want to hurt him? Lord, he'd never understand the ways of women.

Turning off the trail into the trees to give Red a drink, he saw a crude scaffolding fashioned in the lower limbs of an old, bent alder, and looking closer, he saw the leather thongs weathering loose from a tattered red and white blanket, which in turn revealed the weather-stained bones of an Indian who had died an honorable death, which at least implied that he'd lived an honorable life.

A tattered nest of bones, remnants of a man unknown and by now forgotten. Another winter of wind and snow, and the monument of himself would return to the earth and become nothing except everything once again.

Returning to the trail, he thought he should be finding a split oak shake branded with the Irish cross fairly soon.

The countryside was changing. A long time ago, the glacier had dug in deeper here and rolled up more rocks to leave behind when the ice age ended. The trail bed itself became as hard as a cobblestone lane, and he reined Red down to a steady walk to save his feet.

Strange rocky country. Grass didn't like it; he noticed the poisonous larkspur did. Tough brush and gnarled trees eked out a meager hard living, but the good ground lay behind.

Hardly call it cow country, he mused as he rode along, but then he reckoned it would change again and turn into a pretty little valley off yonder.

Coming around a sharp turn, almost a cliff of granite, he saw the branded shake on a wagon wheel propped up against some rocks. Like everything else unattended, it, too, was weathering away and was half-buried in sand that had been banked there by the spring flood of Yellow Creek.

With a sigh of relief, he turned Red up the stream, which didn't look yellow at all, but which seemed to carry the smell of sulfur.

It was still too rocky for good forage, and the surrounding hills were shaly, eroding and slipping before grass seed or root could get a toehold.

Occasionally he passed by a boggy spot that grew grass, but the most of it was rocks, gravel, washed sand, and stunted scrub.

Sam's face gradually became as bleak as the landscape, and when he came to the ranch headquarters, he wasn't too surprised to find the beginnings of a pole barn on a wide, gravelly flat, and little else.

From somewhere on up the canyon, a sulfur spring fed into the creek, making the water almost undrinkable, and the idea of a future ranch here impossible.

Red turned his nose up at the sulfur water, and Sam had to scout around and find a small feeder brook that ran pure. Afterward, he picketed the big horse in a low area where there was enough feed to last the night.

Laying his blanket by his saddle on a flat sandbank, and finding an old fire pit nearby, Sam walked over the flat area, more out of curiosity than anything else.

For him the place was not only hopeless, it was ominous, because banker Elam Castor must have known all along what it was and had deliberately sent him off on a wild-goose chase.

But why?

Why at the last minute, just before he planned to ride upriver?

And Zink had backed him up.

Something rotten was festering in Elk City. He didn't know just yet what it was, but he damned sure meant to find out.

There was nothing of value left behind here. The pile of rubbish off to one side contained a few broken bottles and rusted utensils, which only proved the white man had stayed here. Higher up on the slope were three grave markers, but Sam didn't bother to go up and look.

Probably there was a trace of gold in the creek, and old man McSwayne had thought it was so rich, he'd hide it under the disguise of a cattle ranch, not realizing that all these creeks in the territory had been prospected by the old-timers years ago.

But what did it profit him to ride so far and see so little? He'd wasted a precious summer month depending on the townsmen to do what he should have been doing all along.

It was done. He'd return tomorrow, hand in his badge, and start crisscrossing the country from the Big Horn Mountains to the Crazies if he had to until he found what he wanted and could pay for it.

The smaller downriver ranches were being gobbled up rapidly by the international cattle corporations.

In another year the best of southern Montana would be gone.

He fixed a simple supper of bacon and biscuit, then laid his head on the hard shell of his saddle and watched the stars turn slowly on their infinite wheel.

There hadn't been a sign of Indian activity, and he had no worries about grizzlies or wolves because there was nothing in this desolate valley to attract them.

He lay back on his saddle blanket and let his thoughts roam back to the ranch down in Texas. A long time ago it had been part of a Mexican hacienda, but when Santa Ana was driven south and peace was made, Pa had taken up a piece of it big enough to keep them all riding seven days a week.

Then the terrible war had come, and even if they didn't own any slaves, didn't raise cotton or cane, and in fact had only contempt for landowners and overseers who didn't know their own land, still Pa was bound to join up, and when he was killed, Sam heard of it out in Colorado and had no choice except to volunteer.

Home. What a big world was held in that one little word. The Texas ranch had always been a struggle to break even on, and yet that battle had cemented them all together tighter 'n pups in a basket. The big old house, with the dogtrot in the middle hung with saddles and bridles, had been a kind of heaven to him when he'd come back from the war. The big table in the cookhouse end of the house was the gathering place where they not only had their meals, but where they'd work on guns or leather, or the women would sew, or Ma would read them Psalms from the Bible, things that made life bigger than the hind end of a cow.

They'd played cards on that table, and in bad weather butchered out a critter a half at a time on it, and early on Ma had taught them reading and writing at that same old plank table, which had been the real heart of the ranch.

They'd paid on the mortgage after every fall roundup and figured that was normal business, but once the market was full of mavericks, the price of beef dropped so low, it didn't pay to drive them to market.

That was the year Ma died, and the first year they'd ever missed a payment on the mortgage. The next year hadn't been any better, so the banker, a northerner who'd taken over the old bank, just up and said, "Move on, all of you."

They gave him the land, and they gave him the home, but they rounded up three thousand head of cattle that didn't belong to him and drove them clear to Virginia City, Montana, and sold out.

Buddy had brought up the second section of the herd, about a thousand head, with five other punchers. He was supposed to sell out, bank the money, and come on over to Elk City.

That was the plan, but it wasn't working. Buddy was almost two weeks late already.

Sam awakened from his world of unfulfilled dreams as the first ray of pink touched the white mountain peaks in the east. He was not in the best of moods because he knew now that he'd not only wasted his time, he'd been euchred by the townsfolk.

Nothing for it but to retrace his path, draw his pay, and move on upriver.

After a cup of coffee, he felt more cheerful, and after a breakfast of bacon and mush and some dried apples, he felt almost human.

This valley was bad for the spirit, he decided, and after catching Red and cinching down his leathers, Sam decided to get the hell out of the ghostly place before it spoiled his breakfast.

Within half an hour, and before the sun lifted over the mountains, he was already at the fork of Yellow Creek on the Elk River Trail. Red seemed as pleased as he was to get clear of the rocky, hard valley where the three graves remained as testaments to greed.

He glanced down at the Irish cross burned into the oak shake, and thought how strange it was that McSwayne would pick the one brand that would describe his death best, because when you got right down to it, he had double-crossed himself.

He held the big red gelding there at the fork for a moment, undecided as to which way to go.

Naturally he'd ride on back to Elk City, but he felt impelled to try to make something good out of this trip, and decided to go on west awhile just to see what was there.

Reining Red to the right, he let the big horse go at a stiff trot for a mile, warming him up, and then, because he was so strong, he let him loose on an easy gallop for another mile where the trail curved back toward the river, and the earth became springy again with old sod. Another mile and he was in a big, open pasture that sloped up toward the northern mountains.

This was still reservation land, although the Sioux had moved farther on north.

He brought the sweating sorrel down to a walk and felt better at just seeing so much grass, even if it wasn't his and never would be.

Coulees drained the higher ground, guiding little creeks across the big pasture, and making the kind of paradise he was looking for.

It was completely natural, grass and trees, a few deer and antelope standing still and staring, and nothing else.

Yet as he stopped to survey the area, he caught a discordance out of the corner of his eye that didn't jibe with the rest of the landscape.

He kneed Red over a few feet off the trail and saw a rag of faded blue flannel caught in a clump of bear brush.

He thought it was nothing, just a rag lost by a passing pilgrim, but then his eye picked up a faint sparkle, a glint of yellow, catching the rising sun in the grass.

Curious now, he kneed Red on over and saw the remains of a battered kossuth hat with an army corps badge made of white and blue enamel centering crossed swords. It was the badge of General Phil Sheridan's cavalry corps, and Sam knew it well, because he'd taken the hat and the corps badge off a dead trooper in northern Virginia years before.

Later on he'd worn that hat, for want of any other, fighting down in Tennessee, and when he'd made it home, he'd given it to Buddy as a practical souvenir.

Sam's heart sank as he dismounted and picked up the ragged, sun-faded hat. He had no doubt in his mind that it was Buddy's even if there hadn't been a long red hair stuck inside it.

The blue rag. The hat. And Buddy two weeks overdue.

Searching through the tall grass and small brush, he found more remnants of clothing, torn and discolored, and then he found a boot with its brass gooseneck spur still attached low on the heel. This spur, too, came out of the war, part of the small plunder he'd managed to conserve and bring home. There would be another nearby.

A few yards farther he found a patch of flattened grass where the coyotes and vultures had fought over the flesh of his brother.

He knew it was that way, but he couldn't fit the picture into his head. Sam knew violent death as well as anyone, but it was impossible to envision his brother Buddy as being such a victim out here in the middle of a green nowhere.

Bit of long, reddish hair scattered about, and the bones not yet taken away. The obscene aitchbone. The eyeless horror of the skull. The rib cage still intact and secured to the backbone except where a heavy bullet had busted the spine and carried it on out the sternum.

Ai ai ai! The pain in his heart stopped his breath, and the tears in his eyes fell away blindly and unnoticed.

Here was the other boot and spur, here was his belt and six-gun. Here was his oversize leather wallet, which still held a letter of credit from the Virginia City Bank. Here a few scattered pieces of silver money from his purse. Here a leg bone gnawed by a mouse . . .

6

Laying out his yellow slicker, Sam piled the bones and rags in the center. When he was sure that he had gathered every last scrap, he made a bundle and tied it securely with a length of buckskin thong.

He had no kind of digging implement with him, and only a small hatchet.

He wanted to get away. He wanted to break his hand hitting a tree. He wanted to retch. He wanted to scream at heaven to a God that had wreaked violence on his good family too many times. In the end, he settled down by the oilcloth package and said a little prayer explaining that Buddy never harmed anyone and he'd see him by and by.

The awful hole in the backbone, and even bigger in the front ribs . . . !

Someone had bushwhacked Buddy right out in the open for nothing. No reason at all. He hadn't been robbed. He hadn't been beaten. He'd simply been shot in the back from a safe distance. Why?

When?

Had it something to do with Castor and Zink sending him off on a wasted trip?

He guessed the body had been there at least a week. Maybe ten days.

Assuming Buddy was killed right at this spot, where had the bushwhacker stationed himself?

He stood and looked at the surrounding country. Buddy would be coming up the trail toward Elk City, so the rifleman must have been to the west, off the trail enough not to be seen, yet close enough to see everyone who passed by.

There was a rise that dropped off into a coulee, and on the brow of the rise was a patch of brush and the snag of an old, lightning-blasted pine tree.

Tying the grim bundle behind his saddle, Sam rode directly up the slope to the pine snag, and as he dismounted, saw where a bush had been cut out, leaving a bare, empty place adequate for a man to sit and wait. A knife-cut forked stick that made a good rest for a long rifle had been left behind, and a man's horse could be well hidden out of the way in the yonder coulee.

On hands and knees, he examined the hidden lookout and found nothing until, pawing through the duff at the perimeter of the vacant area, he dug out a long, tubular brass cartridge case. It was stamped .45 on the base of the shell, with the letter R for rifle above it.

From the size of it, Sam guessed it was the powerful .45-120-550 cartridge developed for the long Sharps rifle, and was capable of killing a man at more than eight hundred yards, about half a mile away.

Putting the cartridge case in his breast pocket, Sam remounted and, quietly weeping, rode back down the trail toward Elk City.

As he rode along, he knew he couldn't take those bones to Elk City.

It was almost too much for him. Tears still rolled down

his face, and his eyes were glazed with dull, aching sorrow.

Red moved along at a slow trot, his own spirit seemingly subdued by the pathos and tragedy that rode his back.

Toward noon, Sam came to that point where he'd turned off the day before to water at the river, and pulled up Red as he considered a vagrant idea that passed through his mind.

Settled, he turned Red toward the river again until they came into the clean timber by the rippling clear water, and where the remains of the Sioux nested up in the limbs of the old alder.

Without dismounting, Sam rode directly to that arboreal bier, reached back and untied the yellow bundle behind his saddle, hoisted it up into the boughs of the tree alongside the scaffold of the Indian, and used his doubled-up lariat to make it secure for as long as good horsehair tightly bound together would last.

He reckoned it didn't make any difference now. Not to Buddy, not to anyone. Those bones and scraps of hair and cloth weren't Buddy; they were human relics that needed a tranquil, hallowed place to rest, a place safe from further desecration, and then let them return in nature's own good time to the earth, insubstantial and harmonic.

He could not leave without some serious utterance, not so much to help Buddy along his infinite trail, but to cleanse his own spirit of the fetid sickness that fouled it at this moment.

"Dear Lord, I can't say how hard I feel right now about this, but I want to make it up to Buddy, and make it up to You, too, because the man that killed my brother like that killed a little piece of You, too. I just want to say out loud that whatever it takes, I mean to make it up, because I can't do nothin' else and still call myself a man. . . .

"Now, Red," he said after a moment, "we're goin' to Elk City just as fast as you can make it."

Wheeling the big horse back to the trail, he pointed him upriver, leaned forward, and gripped his knees tightly, giving the signal that the horse had been wanting all along.

Springing forward, Red came out on a long lope, with his great stride eating up the miles, while Sam kept his weight forward, giving him the best ride he could.

There was no more sightseeing along the way. It was simply a matter of letting the big red horse run as hard as he could.

At dusk, trotting the last mile to give Red a chance to cool down, Sam had time to think of his next move.

Right now he had nothing more than the brass cartridge case to go on, and there were thousands of rifles along the trail that accepted that cartridge.

Could it possibly be tied in with the banker Castor sending him off with a false story? Had the banker known of Buddy's murder? Had Castor wanted him to find Buddy's remains?

Nothing seemed to add up right.

Sam turned Red over to Milt Koberman in the livery barn with a request for an extra measure of oats, then walked over to the marshal's office, carrying his saddle-bags over his shoulder.

The street was only partially lighted from coal oil lamps burning in the saloons and the mercantile.

Through the window he saw Jean Louise showing a customer the latest version of the charcoal-burning sadiron. When she saw him pass by the window, she quickly turned away, a gesture that only compounded his confusion and renewed the hurt in his heart.

Damn it, he'd promised Ma to look after the little ones, and that's what he was going to do, even if he'd lost Buddy already. He wasn't going to let any woman get in the way of finding Buddy's murderer and staking him out on an anthill.

Entering the marshal's office, he was surprised to see banker Castor and Randolph Jack talking to Skofer, who was standing by the old rolltop desk.

Castor looked up warily as Sam went on by, opened the door of his sleeping quarters, tossed his saddlebags onto his bunk, then turned back to face the group.

"You're back early," Elam Castor said noncommittally.

"There wasn't enough grass to feed my horse," Sam replied, eyeing the frog-breasted banker with distaste.

"Of course, I've never been there myself"—the banker slipped on his gila monster smile—"but folks have told me it's mighty pretty country."

"Somebody's lyin'."

"Doubtless my informants," Castor said. "Still, you've had a sort of paid vacation, so your time hasn't been completely lost."

Sam was tempted to tell them about finding Buddy's remains, but he thought it would be better to talk it over with Skofer first and break it to him as easy as he could.

"You've gotten back too late," Randolph Jack complained. "If you'd been on duty, you might have stopped the stage robbery."

"Go on," Sam said, feeling a sinking in his belly. Somehow things were coming at him too fast, as if he were one of them circus fellows standing in front of a board while the knife thrower starts to work.

"Just east of town at the crossing. We don't know how many there were, because they killed the driver and the guard," Randolph Jack said.

"They put up a fight?"

"No one knows because there's no one alive to talk," banker Castor said heavily.

"They was each one set down on the ground and shot

through the back of the head," Skofer declared nervously. "I went out there and looked."

"Any tracks, a trail or anything?"

"We lost their tracks in the timber," Skofer said.

"They took a large amount of money that I had entrusted to the stage company only a few minutes before," Castor added.

"I expect they'll pay you back," Sam said.

"I'll see that they do," Randolph Jack said firmly, as if he'd already taken the case to the judge and jury.

"Skofe and me'll go out there first thing in the mornin'," Sam said. "Sounds like newcomers to me . . ."

"How do you mean?" Castor asked.

"Westerners don't just shoot men in the back of the head whilst they're sittin' down."

"Like short-range bushwhackin', that's what it is." Skofer nodded, his Adam's apple bobbing.

"Who found them?" Sam asked.

"It happened I was going upriver to look at a piece of property. Once I saw how it was, I turned right around and reported it to your deputy," Castor said.

"That's right," Skofer stammered, his face flushing red.

"The barber has laid out the bodies, and Reverend Ellison will send 'em off tomorrow," Randolph Jack said piously.

"I doubt we'll be here," Sam said. "I want to stop these killers before they think we're easy pickin's."

"They'll be halfway to Missouri by now," Randolph Jack said, stroking his curly black sideburns.

After Castor and Jack had gone, Skofer paced up and down the room nervously. "I'm sure glad you're back, Captain. I was just about ready to take up serious drinking."

"Settle down, Skofe, I got to tell you somethin' serious, bad news. . . ."

"Buddy?" Skofer murmured, keeping his eyes on Sam's face.

"You knew?"

"I've had a sorrowful feelin' for a week." Skofer nodded.

"He wasn't robbed or nothin'. He was just plain out shot in the back."

"You buried him already?"

"After a week, wasn't much point in bringin' him here."

"That's a hard thing to do, Sam." Skofer's eyes were big, his hands trembled, his mouth worked nervously.

"Steady on. It's almost over. I just want to roast the son of a bitch that did it over a small fire."

Daybreak found them on the upriver trail that turned south only three miles from Elk City and crossed a wide, shallow ford of the river.

"Likely when they slowed down to make the crossing, those jaspers rode out of the timber and took 'em by surprise," Skofer said as they rode through the dawn.

Coming up on the ford, Sam stopped in the timber. "I don't want the tracks messed up any more than they already are," he cautioned, and led Skofer on foot to the edge of the river.

There were the wheel tracks, but the loose sand and gravel from the spring high water wouldn't hold a clear hoofprint.

"Saul Carter, the driver, and the shotgun, old Ben Kamsler, was set down right here." Skofer indicated two separate patches of bloody sand.

"Find the brass?"

"I did." Skofer dug two shell casings from his vest pocket.

Sam looked them over carefully.

"Both .45s," Skofer said.

"But fired from two different revolvers." Sam nodded. "The firing pins struck the primers different."

"So they was at least two of them."

"Saul Carter and Ben Kamsler were tough and experienced. They wouldn't have stopped for anything less 'n four."

"It's mighty hard to hide four coyotes like that in this empty country, Sam," Skofer croaked as if he couldn't fetch out the words that were thought out well enough.

"It's true. Some trapper or prospector would come across four mean jaspers and spread the word."

"Maybe they're killin' anyone that sees 'em," Skofer suggested. "Maybe Buddy saw them together and knew they weren't regular cowpunchers."

"Maybe, but he wasn't killed with a short cartridge."

Sam led the way back to the horses and rode across the river to the opposite bank, where he dismounted and searched again for tracks.

Nodding to himself, he mounted Red and said, "Two of 'em waited over here in case Saul and Ben tried to make a run for it. Likely the others came in on either side as Saul slowed down at the ford. They had him boxed four ways."

Riding back across the river, Sam stopped near the blood-blackened sand and looked around one more time.

"They wouldn't go into town. They wouldn't go north because they'd hit the rocky scree. They either crossed the river and went south or they went upriver. What do you think?"

"Sweet Jesus, I can't even guess," Skofer protested.

"Then we start tryin' to cut their trail both ways. You take the south. Look for a sign. I'll do the same thing upriver."

"Sign?" Skofer asked, puzzled.

"Horseshit. Fresh horseshit. You see any, come tell me," Sam said. "That's one thing they can't hide."

"Count on me, Sam." Skofer grinned, pleased with himself, and rode back across the ford, where he commenced a zigzag course that had the trail as its center line.

Satisfied that Skofer knew what he was doing, Sam headed into the timber and rode north to the scree, looking for any kind of sign, then back to the river on an angle, then back toward the rocky foothills again.

As Sam rode along, he considered that they were almost a full day behind the gang of killers, who could ride hard and fast because they knew where they were going, but for a man to follow their trail, he'd have to go at a walk.

It could be done, though, he thought. Not only could be done, it had to be done.

He hadn't known either Ben or Saul very well, because they only stopped for a few minutes on their weekly run, but what he'd seen, he'd liked. They were decent men, hard-driving and sometimes hard-drinking and hard-living, like most everyone else on the frontier, but they were dead honest, and they had a smile, and if a man was broke down or set afoot, they'd not turn away from him.

There were tracks in the duff, scattered and unreliable, but no fresh sign.

He smiled to himself as he wondered if this bunch was slick enough to train their horses not to shit. Nope, you'd have to be slicker 'n bear grease to do that.

He'd covered half a mile on his easterly base line before he found scattered horse buns. The rider hadn't even let the horse stop, so that the scattered dung made a line, which Sam appreciated. It was like giving him a compass course as to where they were heading.

He dismounted and broke open one of the packed

buns. It was still wet inside, and it smelled fresh enough to suit him.

Turning back, he met Skofer near the main trail.

"Wasn't nothin' fresh," Skofer said, downcast. "Least-wise, I couldn't find it.

"You did fine. It wasn't there. It's up yonder. They're goin' hell-bent upriver."

=== 7 ===

RIDING EAST, SAM WONDERED WHAT WAS EATING THE GUTS of men such as Zink and Castor. Sure as hell, something was changing their ordinary ways. Like most everyone else, they were greedy, but now they seemed almost sick with it, as if they were afraid they were going to lose something valuable.

"Folks in the money business think it's important." Sam smiled over at Skofer. "They figure just plain ordinary life is hardly worth counting."

"Them folks have to start thinkin' different," Skofer croaked, wishing he'd filled his canteen with something stronger than water. "We've taken the land away from the Indians, and now we have to live up to it."

"Couldn't have said it better," Sam said, "but Castor and Zink don't care beans about the land. They'd spit tobacco juice all over it if they thought it would raise their bank balance."

"I figure if you spit in the sky, you're goin' to get it back in your face." Skofer grinned, showing his worn-down teeth.

58

"You s'pose that type of person goes to hell and gets a special punishment?"

"No, I don't, but they'll be just as dead as everybody else and their trash, too."

"Shucks, I was hopin' for some kind of justice." Sam smiled.

"It's a justice, but it takes longer than a man's life," Skofer said. "The justice comes back on the kids. The children and grandchildren pay for the sins of their fathers."

This particular stretch was dotted with big old ponderosa pines and smaller brush, and the going was easy.

They rode parallel for over an hour, with Sam moving back and forth to check the trail and make sure it didn't get littler and littler until it ran up a tree and disappeared.

This country had not really been pacified. The Blackfeet had moved, but there was no telling if they'd come back or not. It depended on how badly the smallpox epidemic took its toll of the once powerful and hard-fighting tribe.

It was pristine, a primitive virgin area of buffalo grass and grama only recently abandoned by the hunting people, and there were still a few beaver left, and always the deer, antelope, and the huge red-coated elk.

The buffalo, though, were gone, and this left the feeder valleys deep in grass, ready and waiting for the wave of cattle coming up from Texas and Missouri and Kansas.

It was one of these valleys that backed up to the Absarokas that Sam had envisioned as his home place.

Yet the country was still too new to just go out and stake a piece of it and say, *This is mine.* You had to go through the proper bureaucratic procedures to make your preemption valid, and this was how the big cattle companies in the East were beating out the smaller local outfits. They could do their business in Washington, laying out their graft, and getting back the papers on the distant lands in exchange—the legislator, bureau hack, or company management never seeing the land or knowing what it really meant to the nation, or how it fit into the scheme of the world.

It was this double problem that Sam was trying to solve. Old Buck Bohannan had solved the bureaucracy paper puzzle, but he hadn't been able to solve the Indian problem, and so had had to leave. Now he didn't want to go back, he just wanted a few dollars for his title and then let him die in a rocking chair on the front porch of a St. Louis rooming house.

Sam kept his eyes on these feeder valleys. Each one had a clear stream running down the middle of it, and each one was big enough to support a thousand beeves year in and year out.

He resolved to go on over to Miles City as soon as he had the time and check these long feeder valleys to see if the eastern corporations had gobbled them up yet.

They were moving along steadily at a good trot and occasionally passing over open ground where hoofprints showed up clearly, and Sam was certain he was trailing three of the possible four outlaws, but there were other odd prints that seemed to not belong.

Remembering Buddy, Sam tried to watch for points of ambush, not only for himself, but Skofer, too, but nothing interfered with their pursuit until the sun was in the west and Sam was thinking of making camp.

The richness of the rising river valley touched a chord in Sam's memory. Compared to the thorny scrub of Coleman County, where he'd grown up pulling stickers out of his hands and arms every day, and dust from working the cattle caked a man's sweating face so that he looked to be masked in mud, this ground was like a dream of childhood where everything was green, the grass like the sea surf, the water burbling along clean and bountiful, and the air pure as a bluebird's eye.

Course, it got cold in winter and a man would need to put up with the blizzards, but it couldn't be no colder 'n a blue norther blowing across Texas in January. That kind of cold froze the marrow in your bones and set you shaking with the ague.

Suddenly, from over a low rise of a knoll, came the crack of a rifle, followed by a fusillade of gunfire from farther on up the rolling hills.

Sam drove Red forward in front of Skofer's buckskin, thinking at first that they were the targets, but there was no spinning scream of rifle balls coming near, and he checked Red, stood in his stirrups, and motioned Skofer to hold and be quiet.

After the first volley, the gunfire became sporadic, coming from different areas except for the steady crashing of a repeater, probably a Spencer by the sound of it, Sam thought.

"Somebody's pinned down," Sam said in a low voice to Skofer. "Hold the horses while I take a look."

Hauling his own .44-40 Winchester from its boot, Sam dismounted and commenced to snake his way up the rise.

Reaching the crest, concealed in the tall grass, Sam took off his hat and rose to one knee, looking off up the side hill where the timber started.

The pinned-down man, protected by a fallen log, might retreat into the denser timber if he wanted, but so far he preferred to hold his ground.

From the farther knoll, a rifleman was pecking away at the log, with little effect. Over to the right and lower down, another rifleman was wasting his ammunition, and maybe fifty yards directly below Sam, another rifleman was doing the same thing. They had the hombre in a three-way hitch, but they needed a fourth to hold him, if that's what they wanted.

Behind the pinned-down man, far back in the woods, Sam caught a glimpse of a pale horse and a white mule.

Cain King. Of course. The White Bear. The King of Death. That's why he wasn't running away. He was on the attack. He wanted a body for bounty.

From Sam's viewpoint, he could see that King had three rifles stacked against the log and a Spencer at his shoulder, and he was picking his shots carefully, all directed at the man off to his left.

Farther up-valley Sam could see how the land changed as a solid rock dike extended across the upper throat of the valley, broken only by a jagged cut for the river to pass through.

That, then, must be the gap, and Bohannon's Bench had to be just beyond it, Sam realized.

Shots continued sporadically, but the man below Sam was moving off to the left, snaking through the grass and brush so as to get a shot at King's blind side.

Sam heard a noise behind him and quickly turned with his rifle, only to see that it was Skofer sneaking up alongside him.

"You was supposed to stay with the horses," Sam whispered grimly.

"They're safe, but hidin' don't set right with me." Skofer poked his head up to see what was going on.

"Stay down!" Sam punched his big hand into Skofer's back, driving him flat to the grass. "You'll get yourself a hole in the head playin' the prairie dog," Sam growled.

"I'm sorry, Sam," Skofer whispered meekly.

"Don't be sorry, just keep your head down." Sam smiled, and saw how the rifleman below him moved a few feet every time King fired at the man on his left. Bit by bit, the rifleman below was making for a rock where he'd have a perfect shot at King's back.

"You think they're the jaspers we're lookin' for?" Skofer asked.

"I'm thinkin' they're ready to run for Bohannon's Bench as soon as they can let go of the White Bear's tail," Sam murmured.

He couldn't be sure the three sharpshooters were the same men who had robbed the stage. Likely they were, but he couldn't back-shoot any of them, no matter how vicious they were.

He had no use for the White Bear, even though he was helping to clean up the country with all the strength and cunning of a newly converted zealot.

But for sure he couldn't set back and watch the man below him cross over behind King and just bushwhack him in cold blood.

The man gained the security of the lone rock protruding from the hillside, and proceeded to lay the barrel of his long rifle, probably a Springfield, Sam thought, in a cleft of the rock and slowly draw a bead on King's huge, buckskin-clad back.

Sam wasn't ready, but he had to give warning. Rising to his knees, he quick-aimed and snapped a slug off toward the man behind the rock.

The rifle fired into the air, and the man dived for cover.

Skofer, unable to control his curiosity, rose on his knees to look even as Sam was falling on his belly.

The shot from over to the right cracked through the limpid air and knocked Skofer flat on his back.

"Oh! Sam . . ." he groaned, putting his hand to his upper left arm and looking at the blood, "Sam, I done it again."

"Hold still," Sam whispered, and crawled close to Skofer, his head an inch above the ground as more heavy bullets screamed and spanged over the knoll.

Taking Skofer by the upper right arm, Sam dragged him slowly back through the tall bluestem downhill.

Skofer was biting his lip to keep from crying out at the pain, and Sam murmured, "Ease off now, I know it smarts some, but it won't kill you."

Sam examined the wound and checked to make sure the bone wasn't broken, then bound his bandanna tight around the wound and waited for the blood to clabber up and commence repairs.

"Darn it," Skofer said, "you oughta hit me, Sam."

"Whatever for?" Sam pretended to be a lot cheerier than he felt. He wanted to make sure the three sharpshooters were the stage robbers and the killers of Ben and Saul. He'd wanted to take them in for a quick trial and hanging, but it wasn't going to be that way now.

He had to get Skofer back to Elk City before the shock and loss of blood made him unable to ride at all. Sam found the horses tethered to a fallen pine snag and led them back to where Skofer lay quietly.

"C'mon, trooper, we're goin' back to Elk City and find us a sawbones."

"I should have listened to you, Sam." Skofer hung his head. "I never thought they'd take a shot at me."

Sam heard the firing over the hill change directions, and there seemed to be a movement, a change in positions as the three sharpshooters shifted places.

"Sounds like they're pulling around into Bohannon's Bench," Sam said, "but old White Bear, he's hangin' on to them like a sticktight."

Helping Skofer up on the buckskin, Sam mounted Red, and aimed downriver in a straight line. He knew now where Bohannon's Bench was, and he'd be better prepared when he returned. At least one question was answered. When the young gunsels passed through town and went upriver, he knew now where they planned to stay.

Yet another question had fallen on top of the answer. Who was that fourth man who had split off from the others after killing Saul and Ben?

Skofer was near to falling out of the saddle by the time they reached Elk City after dark. Sam rode close alongside him, his right hand gripping him about the waist as they made their way slowly down Main Street. There were few people on the street, and those few were already stumbling from one saloon to another, uncaring about anything except finding another horn of red liquor.

Sam brought them up to the hitch rail in front of the doc's office, lifted Skofer out of the saddle, and gently set him to the ground. Then gripping him around the waist without any protest from Skofer, he helped him walk to the boardwalk and knocked on the door.

In a minute, the door opened and a small man with a white beard, old Doc, peered out into the darkness. "Who is it?"

"Sam Benbow, Doc, and Skofer. Skofer needs some attention."

Sam helped Skofer move forward into the front room, which served as the doctor's office.

Lighting a pair of lamps with shiny reflectors, Doc said, "Lay him down on the cot."

Sam put Skofer down and helped him stretch out.

"Caught the lower shoulder and the arm, eh?" Doc said briskly, then with a pair of scissors, cut away Skofer's shirt and Sam's bandanna bandage.

It was a bloody mess turning blue, but Doc swabbed around the edges of it until he could see its dimension.

"Lucky for you, old-timer, you'll be able to keep your shoulder working. If blood poisonin' sets in, then we'll just bury you and forget your name," Doc announced cheerfully.

"I hope you're a better doctor than the last one I went to," Skofer said grimly.

"I've got a good record." Doc smiled. "Even my first case was successful."

"And what kind of a case was that?" Skofer asked skeptically.

"It was a birthing. The baby died, the mother died, but I managed to save the father," Doc said.

"It figures," Skofer squawked as the doctor applied a purple solution of permanganate acid to the wound.

"Now, what were you saying about your last doctor?"

"It was a simple case," Skofer said. "A lady I knew rather well said I slept with my mouth open. So I went to the doctor and told him my problem. He pondered awhile and said it was incurable. Said my skin was extra short, so every time I closed my eyes, my mouth opened."

"I must remember that." Old Doc nodded and dabbed more permanganate on the gash. "Medical science advances so swiftly, it's hard to keep up."

Sam looked from one to the other and shook his head disgustedly. "You're both the biggest liars since Davy Crockett. Now, just tell me, is it a clean wound or not?"

"He never did have a sense of humor." Skofer winked at the doc.

"Yes it is, Sam," Doc said, looking up. "Goin' to ache like hell and itch for a month, but it'll heal. I won't sew on it any because I think the pain ain't worth the bother. But I am goin' to tie it up as tight as I can, and I want Skofer to keep it that way until I tell him different."

"Yes, sir," Skofer said obediently.

"I'm goin' to charge you a two-dollar idiot fee so you'll learn to keep away from bullets."

"How about a discount for half-wits?" Skofer closed his eyes tiredly.

"That's no joke," Sam said.

"You stay here tonight so I can look at you first thing in the mornin'," the wiry old medico advised. "Hear me?"

"God . . ." Skofer murmured from a worried dream, and breathed deeply.

"That's the kind of patient I like." The old doctor nodded. "Knows when it's time to rest."

"Thanks, Doc," Sam whispered, patted the old man's bony shoulder, and went on out into the street.

After he'd turned the horses over to old Milt Koberman in the livery barn, he strolled slowly up to the

Bonny Kate, his legs stiff from so much walking during the day.

Man wasn't meant to walk because God give him the horse, Sam thought as he paused at the batwing doors to make sure he wasn't walking into a hornet's nest.

Herman was playing his accordian, Madeline and Dixie sat at a table at the end of the bar nursing watered-down drinks and eyeing him coolly as he came in. He noticed Randolph Jack and another dude conferring at a table in the corner.

Of the other men hunkered over the bar, he recognized only Edward Starbuck and a couple older cowpunchers who, like Sam, were looking for a home.

The older punchers had no complaint. They'd played what cards were dealt out to them, and though they might dream of the home ranch, they'd not worry about the bunkhouse and small wages until something went wrong, and that became worrisome if you ever let yourself think about it. Because if the big company ranch you had given your best to didn't want you anymore because your leg was broke or your piles bleedin' and keepin' you out of the saddle, you were going to end up worse 'n Milt Koberman. These eastern companies, they didn't much like feeding the old men or the cripples. You look for the boss of the Durham Cattle and Land Company, and find out there ain't such a man nowhere, it's a bank.

But these older punchers at the bar weren't thinking that far ahead. They were in town to pick up supplies for some distant outfit, and they'd be gone tomorrow. With any luck they'd be hung for rape when they were ninety years old.

Coming to the bar, Sam said to Pat Duveen, "Glass of that good Tennessee Mountain special."

Pat poured a double measure in the glass and asked conversationally, "See anything of those jaspers?"

"Not sure. Saw somebody. They winged Skofer, and I had to break off and bring him in."

The whiskey was soft and had a smooth way of going down, then releasing its warmth to unravel the nerves and ease the tired muscles.

"Ah! The bold lawman!" Edward Starbuck turned to see Sam sipping his whiskey. "What hath thou wrought?"

Sam looked over at the small, erect man in his elegant frock coat and gold watch chain, and nodded. "Evenin', sir."

"Greetings and all that rubbish," the small man continued loudly, "but what ho?"

"What ho is my deputy got winged by somebody that maybe was in on the stage robbery."

"Maybe! Somebody! What kind of language is that?"

Sam saw that Starbuck was drunk and overreaching himself with whiskey talk.

"You about ready to wind up the night, Mr. Starbuck?"

"Not at all, my gallant lawman, not at all! You've only just arrived!"

"And I'm about ready to leave," Sam said.

"Tell me, are you maintaining law and order?"

"Are you writin' anything?" Sam rejoined easily.

"Ah, you do dare challenge me! The answer is a resounding affirmative. I am writing today of the false gods, of the mythology of the westerner's derring-do. I am puncturing the hot-air balloon that lifts the so-called western knight errants far above their proper station."

"Sure now, I wish you lots of luck, Mr. Starbuck. I reckon I'll just mosey off to my mythological bunk."

"Ah, don't leave like a craven milksop. Tell me of your adventures first."

"So you can puncture the balloon of hot air?" Sam smiled.

"Only after I weigh the hyperbole that will grow and grow."

"How do you get to be somebody that judges which is which and what is what?"

"One must seize every opportunity."

"Do you sell these writings of yours that puncture the hot-air balloons?" Sam asked evenly.

"I've not yet finished. Once I'm satisfied as to accuracy and style, I'll sell it, all right."

"You mean you can make some money just settin' around saloons?"

"I'm afraid I must," Starbuck said bitterly. "My backer has cut me off without a farthing, but he doesn't yet reckon on my skill with the pen."

"Maybe Mr. Zink'd hire you on and Miss Jean Louise could stay home and keep house," Sam said, not understanding Starbuck's line of blustering talk, although he noticed Randolph Jack listening closely.

"My daughter's name should not be mentioned in this place!" Starbuck came back hotly. "We are not discussing her. We're discussing my involvement."

"Fine with me."

"I'm not finished, young man!" Starbuck stood on his tiptoes, his chin about a foot below Sam's. "I want you to stay away from my daughter. . . ."

"I'm doin' my best," Sam said. "Soon as you're ready to go outside and puke your guts up, I'll help you home."

— 8 —

SAM WAS UP EARLY. HIS FIRST THOUGHT OF THE DAY WAS that it took a special breed to be a lawman. You spend your whole life at it, and if you've been good at the job, nothing has changed. It isn't any better nor any worse, but your own life has gone to serving papers, throwing drunks in jail, pursuing an occasional rustler or killer, but all in all, the effort is futile.

Maybe nothing changes for a rancher, but at least he's working for himself and his family, he's growing something, and with a little luck, the ranch will be a better place when he dies than when he first started.

Lawmen, after a few years of it, seem to have some heavy weight on their minds. They lose their natural smile, and a lot of them turn out to be plain mean.

Whatever it was, he knew the job wasn't good enough for him to spend much of his own life on it, and when he went up the street to Ira's Café, he felt like whistling "Yankee Doodle."

"My, aren't you the early bird!" Sally McKenzie greeted him cheerfully as she put the thick mug of coffee in front of him.

"Still, you're ahead of me." Sam smiled. "How do you manage?"

"It's the rooster," she laughed. "Dad brought him all the way from Fort Riley, and he wakes up an hour earlier than anyone else, sticks his head in my window, and sounds reveille!"

"Where's your dad now?"

"They're bivouacked down by Carson, but they've got orders to come on up into Montana soon. Ham and eggs?"

"Over easy," Sam said, feeling a liking for the spunky girl, even if she was a pest most times. Always cheerful. Even first thing in the morning.

Must have got it travelin' around from one army post to another. The sort of cheeriness that comes from having to adjust to changes whether you like it or not.

Just as Sam was leaving, he met Randolph Jack and the dude friend that had been with him the night before.

"Morning, Marshal," Jack said smoothly. "This is a friend of mine, Hamilton Blasingame from Washington, D.C."

"Glad to meet you," Sam said, taking the slender, soft hand of the thin-chested stranger.

"My pleasure, sir," Hamilton Blasingame replied in a voice that started down at his belly button and commenced reverberating about his breastbone. "I certainly do admire this country and the men who are fighting to pacify it."

"You goin' to be here long?" Sam asked politely.

"Just another day or two. We'll be out looking over the new land—"

Before he could finish, Randolph Jack had a fit of coughing and crowded into the dude, breaking off his sentence, then said, "Yes, well, now let's have a big, country-style breakfast!" with a great show of enthusiasm that left Sam out.

"Good to meet you, Marshal," Blasingame said.

71

"I hope to see you before you leave," Sam replied easily. "You need a guide, maybe I can help out."

"That won't be necessary, Marshal." Jack moved in smoothly again. "Our trip is already well organized."

Sam went on out to the street. It didn't need any bobtailed genius to figure out that Mr. Hamilton Blasingame was in the land investment business and had an office in Washington, D.C., just down the hall from the congressmen who were in charge of distributing the new public domain.

Sam didn't classify Randolph Jack as a deserving landowner. He was just a promoter who would use his influence to gain what others couldn't, and he'd do it just to turn over a fast profit.

It was this type of a system Sam was fighting against. The genuine settler was so discouraged by all the rules and red tape, he'd have to pony up some extra money and buy the same land from such a promoter as Randolph Jack.

Crossing the street to the doctor's office, he found Skofer up and dressed, pacing the floor of the office, alone.

"Sam!" he cried out in relief. "Can I go now? I don't remember all what the doc told me last night."

"We can go, but you'll need to see the doc later on today."

"Bless his heart, he trussed me up like he was set to roast me for a wild turkey." Skofer rolled his eyes and smiled as they went outside.

"Some sore?"

"Some." Skofer nodded. "Nothing a glass of beer won't cure."

"You're goin' to eat, Skofe. No beer." Sam shook his head.

As Skofer went into the café, Sam saw Cain King riding his pale horse and leading his white mule down the street.

It was a curious sight, King with his prematurely white hair and beard looking like one of the many old prospectors riding the trails and panning the distant creeks, but most prospectors had their mules packed with a pick and shovel, maybe some black powder and a gold pan or two. Cain King's mule was packed with firearms.

Sam counted three long scabbards hanging on each side of the tarpaulin-covered pack, and shook his head with wonder.

Crossing over, he followed King into the mercantile, and seeing Jean Louise standing near the door, tipped his hat and said, "Good mornin', ma'am."

Flushing at his formality, she said, "Good morning, Mr. Benbow."

"Looks like it'll be a nice day," Sam offered.

"Did you bring my father home last night?"

"I figured it was my job."

"You have no right to abuse my father," she said distantly.

"I kind of thought it was the other way, ma'am," Sam said. "Next time, if you like, I'll let him sleep it off in the jail."

"That will not do," she said, her eyes like pinpoints of obsidian.

"My feelings exactly. The worst part of my job is cleaning up the cell after the drunks have throwed up all over or worse," he said succinctly.

"You're being vulgar because you're angry with me."

"I reckon your pa, pitiful as he is, is the real vulgar one. Take a look sometime."

"Oh! You're impossible!" she snapped, quickly turned away, and retreated to the back of the women's wear department.

"Yes'm," Sam murmured, and went on back to the rear counter, where King was giving his order to old Mr. Zink.

"Three boxes of the .45-120-550 for my Sharps, five

boxes of .56-50 for the Spencer. Better have four boxes for the .45-70-405 Springfield, and a couple boxes of .44-40 for the Colt pump. Then I'll need about five pounds of powder, a sack of double-ought buck, and a sack of twelve-gauge ball. I guess that'll take care of it."

Zink finished writing down the order, and asked, "You going to kill all the Sioux left? Ha ha!"

"When they put a bounty on Sioux, I'll be up there bringin' 'em in," King growled, and seeing Sam approaching, asked, "That you on the knoll yesterday?"

"Me and Skofer." Sam nodded.

"Much obliged to you for the warnin'."

"Who were those three jaspers peggin' away at you?"

"Only one that I could put a dodger on. Ogden Santee. A slippery cuss worth four hundred dollars if I had of caught him. Used the Colt at first because it was handy, but fell short. Should've hauled out the Sharps and I'da brought him in nice and tidy."

The rich southern drawl coming out of the bearlike man in dirty buckskins still bothered Sam. Somewhere long ago there had been a gentleman inside that battered carcass.

Where had it gone?

"Ogden Santee. He used to operate down around San Antonio, didn't he?"

"That's the one. Killed a few ordinary gunfighters down that way, but got his picture put up for rape and murder of a young lady." The big man smiled grotesquely.

"What do you reckon him and the other two were doin' way upriver?"

"It's an interestin' subject," King said. "There's a million or so acres of land upriver that will open up soon, but these three went on up into Bohannon's Bench. There's no way to get 'em out of there so long as they keep a sharpshooter watchin' the gap."

"You saw 'em ride on into Bohannon's?"

"I followed their tracks right up to where the river breaks through."

"How many you s'pose are holed up in there now?" Sam asked conversationally.

"I'd guess six or eight right now. Give me a hundred dollars apiece and I'll bring 'em in for you." King grinned.

"I don't even know who they are," Sam said tightly, thinking it wasn't too bad of an idea, really. For sure they were owl-hooters fixing to make trouble in the territory, and sooner or later would have to be rooted out.

"Who was that lovely lady you were speaking to?" King asked, as if the thought had just crossed his mind.

"You mean Jean Louise Starbuck? She's goin' to be the new schoolmarm. Why?"

"Thought I might have known her someplace else. . . ." King muttered, turning away and barking at Zink, "Let's get a move on, Mr. Storekeeper, I can't make any money in here."

"I'm short a box of the .56-50," Zink said, looking through the shelf stacked with ammunition.

"Then give me what you've got," King said, and turned back to Sam. "I burned up a hundred dollars worth of cartridges yesterday, and you people won't come near to giving me a decent bounty price. How the hell can you expect a man like me to make a livin'?"

"I'd like to put a bounty on the politicians and Philadelphia lawyers that are tryin' to hog the land," Sam said, his mood changing.

"Hard to catch them kind." King grinned. "But if you can make it worth my while . . ."

"What I'd like to do and what's legal are two different kind of horses." Sam noticed King was staring across the counters at Miss Jean Louise Starbuck on the other side of the store.

"It ain't often I see a real lady," King muttered.

"Where do you camp?" Sam asked on an impulse.

"Why?" King shot back.

"Curious." Sam shrugged.

"Well, if you want to know, I chased a grizzly sow and two cubs out of a cave, and I figure to live there until something bigger 'n me runs me out."

Sam still didn't know any more than he ever did.

"It must be fairly close in, the way you keep track of the trails and folks comin' and goin'."

"How would I go about meetin' a lady like that?" King asked uncertainly, as if hating to ask a favor.

"Two ways. Go over there and buy a new suit of clothes from her, or go down to the Topaz Saloon and buy her father a couple of drinks," Sam said, bitterness creeping into his voice.

Sam turned away before his anger showed, walked out to the boardwalk, and took a breath of fresh air, trying to think of how Buddy's murder was tied up with the rest of the violence. There had to be some connection between Buddy's death and Bohannon's spread being turned into a robbers' roost, but there were too many pieces missing to fit the puzzle together.

His sunny mood had been devoured and buried by the grisly bounty hunter with his sometimes courtly manners, and more often his crazy polecat notion that life was valued according to how much the government was willing to pay somebody to take it away from you.

Wandering along toward the Bonny Kate, he was overtaken and passed by three riders who were distinctive, not so much because they were wearing dude clothes complete with bow ties and derbies, but because they were young and hard, possessing that same feral arrogance that the two youngsters, Lonnie Sackbutt and Frank Arbole, had shown two days before.

As they dismounted and shucked their linen dusters,

Sam saw the swagger, the low-slung blue steel Colts, the unblemished boots, the sneering little smiles.

Sam followed them on into the Bonny Kate.

When they asked Pat Duveen for three beers, Sam went to his favorite place at the end of the bar where he didn't have to worry about his back.

"Coffee," he murmured to Pat as he approached.

"It's extra special today." Pat smiled.

"How's that?" Sam asked, a little perturbed.

"The sack I usually use to hold the coffee grounds had a hole in it, so I had to use Grandma's sock. I don't think she washed it ever in her long life." Pat winked.

"I guess that ought to make it real tasty then." Sam nodded. "But maybe I'd better have some sugar with it."

Pat brought the coffee, and said, "Don't worry about it. Grandma never ever touched soap and water to her feet."

"What'd she do, rub 'em with lard?" Sam asked, deadpan.

"How'd you guess!" Pat hooted with laughter, and brought stares from the three young hardcases on down the bar.

"Hey! What's so funny? You laughin' at us?"

"No, we're laughin' about my grandmother," Pat replied, still so tickled, his broad belly was bobbing up and down like a bumbershoot in a twister. "Lard . . . ! Rub 'em down with lard! Ah, God . . ."

Sam noticed a kind of suicidal madness in their eyes, as if they just might fling out and do anything just to make some action, even if they got killed doing it.

"They ain't laughin' at us, Tommy," the taller one said. "Drink your beer."

"Just askin'," the one called Tommy grumbled.

"Where's the bank?" the tall one with a hatchet-thin face asked Pat Duveen.

"Go out to the boardwalk. Turn right and it's a

red-brick building on the corner. You can't miss it," Pat said cheerfully.

"Screw your grandmother," the third one with the wildest eyes sneered.

"It's a joke," Pat said soberly. "My poor grandmother died in Ireland before I was born."

"Pipe down, Sid," the taller one said in a bleak, hard tone. "I'm about to send you back to the orphanage."

"Where's the whores?" Tommy snarled, ignoring the taller one.

"We don't have whores in Elk City." Pat Duveen folded his hands on his chest and looked up at the ceiling.

"What the hell do you do for fun—flubbity-dubbity?" Sid acted as if he'd made a joke.

"That's enough." The tall, hatchet-faced one threw a new gold coin on the bar. "C'mon, we're gettin' out of here before you get the marshal there riled at us."

"I ain't riled just yet," Sam said. "Some curious, though, boys. Where you from and where you goin'?"

"We're from St. Louis," the tall one said. "My name's Mullins."

"And we're goin' to the bank on private business," Tommy snarled.

"And then you're leavin' town. Goin' upriver, I s'pose?"

"We don't know for sure just where we're goin'," the tall one called Mullins said, and punched Tommy on the shoulder to get him moving.

"I entertained a couple lads from St. Louis a couple days ago. One was called Lonnie, the other Frank," Sam said idly.

"Never heard of 'em," the tall one said, herding his two friends along toward the door.

"Just in case you can't find the bank, let me show you the way," Sam said, following along and going through the batwing doors like one of the group.

"We'll find it," Mullins said.

"Why the hell you keep tryin' to choke him with cream, I don't know," Tommy snarled at Mullins.

"Shut up, Tommy, or go back where you come from," Mullins said, his right hand touching the butt of his low-slung Peacemaker.

"You leave us be. . . ." Tommy turned on Sam.

"I'm just goin' to show you the bank," Sam said, blank-faced, eyeing the small, wild one.

"We got private business in that bank," Mullins said, striding up the boardwalk.

"We always like to show our hospitality to newcomers with money," Sam said, walking along with the three-some.

As they came to the front steps of the bank, the hatchet-faced Mullins said, "Thanks, Marshal. We can find it from here."

"I'll just go along and introduce you to the banker," Sam said. "I've known him almost a month now."

"I say we shoot the nosy bastard." Tommy turned, his arm cocked, his shoulder sloped, his eyes showing white and crazy.

"It upsets my breakfast to kill a kid this early," Sam said levelly, "but you keep makin' talk like that, I'll have to do it and go take a soda pill."

"Move!" Mullins pushed Tommy on up the steps, and with Sam tagging along behind, entered the front door.

Limp-wristed Boze Crowelly was at the teller's window adding up numbers in a ledger, and just beyond the counter was Elam Castor, cleaning his nails with a small jackknife, smiling serenely at his ever-enriching financial world.

"Can I help you?" Boze Crowelly asked as the four approached, ready to dive under the counter and scurry for the back door.

"We want the boss," Mullins said.

"He's occupied at the moment. Can you tell me something of the nature of your business?" Crowelly murmured as if by rote.

Mullins was already walking on down the counter toward Castor's desk, and the banker realized he had business at hand.

Castor looked over the three hardcases and then Sam, bringing up the rear.

"Something I can do for you, Marshal?" the banker asked, putting on his gila monster smile.

"I figured it might be the other way," Sam replied, not backing up.

"I see. And what brings you here, sir?" he asked Mullins.

"You got my letter?"

"You're . . ."

"Jefferson Mullins."

"Oh, yes, Mr. Mullins. Of course . . ."

"Can you get rid of him, or does he stick like a burr on the old cow's tail?" Mullins nodded toward Sam.

"Thank you, Marshal"—the banker beamed—"but these gentlemen and I have some private business to attend to—"

"This the new breed of pioneer?" Sam looked at the three contemptuously.

"The country's big enough for all kinds of people, Marshal. We can't expect everyone to look alike."

Sam was about to mention how Bohannon's Bench was filling up with just this type of look-alike, but thought it better to hold off.

Something was definitely going wrong, and they were treating him like a knotheaded Mormon puke, as if he couldn't smell the rottenness in this room.

"Like they say, Mr. Castor, birds of a feather."

"You are rather famous for your old adages, aren't you, Marshal?" The banker glared at Sam.

"Another one is 'Bad money drives out good.'" Sam grinned and turned away.

"Come here, Barney," Skofer called out to the grizzled airedale. "Time we learned a new tune."

The dog raised his head from the boardwalk warily, got to his feet, and retreated across the street, his shoulders humped over, his head turned so that he could see where he was going and watch Skofer following, too.

"Here, Barney," Skofer coaxed. "I'll buy you a big cow bone if you'll just practice some . . ."

Barney sidled across the dirt street, avoiding a couple passing riders and a lumber dray as well as Skofer, and made it safely over to the opposite boardwalk, where he paused to think it over.

"Come on, Barney," Skofer said softly. "You can sing tenor, and I'll be baritone. We'll do 'Dixie' . . . do it real pretty. . . ."

Barney shook his head and moved down the boardwalk to wait again, this time in front of the batwing doors of the Bonny Kate.

Coming closer, Skofer said, "All right, the war's over. We can do 'Darling Nellie Gray' or 'Flow Gently Sweet Afton,' anything you like, just name it."

The brown dog pondered the proposition a moment, curled his upper lip, and moved on down the boardwalk, leaving Skofer standing in the doorway of the Bonny Kate, where the redolent aroma of spilled beer, tobacco juice, and mildewed sawdust drifted out.

His nose wrinkled and his rubbery lips formed a smile.

"Some other day, Barney," Skofer called. "I just remembered an important engagement."

Pushing his way through the doors, Skofer advanced into the gloom toward the bar with a springy step and a light heart.

"A glass of your finest and oldest Tennessee whiskey,

Mr. Duveen," Skofer said grandly. "Marshal Benbow asks that you put it on his bill."

"Does he now?" Pat smiled, putting a half-full bottle and a glass in front of the wiry gamecock. "Sure, if he complains, I'll refer him to you."

"He will not complain. That young man has ridden through shot and shell with me, and many times I have had to save his life on the field of battle. . . ."

Skofer managed to bobble down two drinks while he was speaking, and then he noticed Cain King the White Bear staring at him.

"Who did you serve under?" King growled, tossing down his own glass of whiskey.

"Captain Benbow and I rode with Jeb Stuart," Skofer said carefully.

"What were you doing?" King pointed a finger at Skofer's bony chest.

"It happens that I was a professor of divinity at the University of Virginia at the outbreak of the war," Skofer murmured, and paused to down another. "I felt it my duty to volunteer as regimental chaplain."

"Chaplain?" King stared at him hard in disbelief. "Don't play games with the King of Death, little man."

"You don't understand. . . ." Skofer said nervously, and poured another. "I went into the war as an academic full of faith, and I came out of it a distant admirer of humanity and with a certain faith in the balm of this precious elixir. . . ." Lifting his glass, he smiled and nodded. "Come join me, I am the king of wine, women, and song."

"I took the post of chaplain after all the others were blown to hell," King growled. "I told the dying boys all the lies that I had learned at my mother's knee, until I finally understood God was mocking me. God was saying death is forever, death is mutilation, blinded eyes, blood-gushing mouths, grinning heads rolling down the grassy hillside, white bones pasted to a tree trunk. Death is God and God is death!"

"Put it behind you," Skofer said. "Why not say God is in every smile, in every joyful moment of love, in every hop jigging around the dance floor, and certainly cheering in this very chalice." Skofer held up the glass, grinned, and drank it down.

"Death is horror and forever!" King cried out, his forehead wrinkled with pain, his tortured lips twisting. "Death is what I breathe in every day, what I drink and eat, what I spew on the land, and the blessing I give you all!"

"I don't think anymore of God in His heaven or the Devil in his hell. Let those two old lawyers grind the armies down to what you want, I shall carry on as Bacchus would have it and play Cupid's game." Skofer laughed. "I'll enjoy what I've salvaged while I can."

"You're a fool!" King thundered. "I am the Destroyer! I am the Lord of Sacrifice! I am the King of Death, and I will avenge the murder of my soul!"

"I say, Mr. Barman," Skofer said, lifting the bottle and squinting his eyes, "doesn't this look like it needs refilling?"

"Not today, Mr. Skofer." Pat Duveen smiled, taking the empty bottle from Skofer's fingers. "I believe Mr. Benbow is waiting for Cupid's assistance."

"Do you really?" Skofer looked at Pat Duveen, his eyes owlly, his knees sagging.

Crossing the street, Sam took the stool closest to the window in Ira's Café and asked Sally for a cup of coffee while keeping his eyes on the bank doorway.

Sally wisely brought the coffee, said nothing, and retreated back to the kitchen, where old Ira was pegging around on his crutch, flipping flapjacks and frying bacon for latecomers.

On the back of the big iron stove, a great enameled pot simmered with extra bones and prairie turnips, sage seasoning, and pepper and salt for the soup stock, and as Sally opened the oven door, she stabbed a broomstraw into the golden brown top of an apple pie and pronounced it done.

"All right," Ira grumbled with a smile, "I guess you know what you're doin'. I'm a steak-and-potatoes man myself."

"Nothing wrong with steak and potatoes," she said with a merry smile, "but apple pie makes a man think of home, and then he thinks of his mother."

"I got you," Ira laughed, "and then he thinks of his sweetheart, right?"

"You're way ahead of me, Sergeant Armsbury," she said, her face flushing a bright red.

"I'll say this. . . ." Old Ira pegged off toward his butcher block, where a hind quarter of beef lay waiting for him to cut it into steaks and roasts. "You could do worse."

"That's as backhanded a compliment as you can make," she retorted.

"All right, if it riles you, I'd say that you couldn't do much better."

"That's more my style." She grinned as she lifted out one of the hot pies and placed it on the counter to cool.

Sam, unaware of the fine silk net being woven only a few feet away from him, sipped his coffee and watched the bank, wishing he could hear what business was being negotiated inside.

The banker had been almost brazen in his welcome of the young gunslingers, as if already he had so much power, nothing could stop him. As if he could eliminate any obstruction by simply nodding his head like a Caesar. Nod your head, and down comes the ax on the troublemaker's neck.

Won't be like that, Mr. Banker, Sam thought. You

don't have a big enough ax yet. Long as I can carry my Peacemaker and have guts enough to use it, you ain't goin' to ax my neck, Mr. Banker.

He had the sudden thought that the best thing for him to do right at that moment would be to go over there and shoot them all. Just do it and wipe off the disease of corruption before it had a chance to start. But, of course, right or wrong, he wouldn't do it because he'd been raised to respect the law.

No, he would abide awhile. Right now all he had was a cloud of suspicions that wouldn't localize into true building blocks that might be called facts or truth. It was all a mass of feelings, and sometimes your feelings could be wrong just because a man wore black instead of brown, or cocked his cigar up instead of down. Feelings were fine if you were totally true to yourself, but too often something in a man's past would spark off the wrong sentiment, and then he was in deep trouble.

For now he'd take a mixture of facts and fancy. He felt that the banker was a spider spinning his web to catch the innocent, and he was nearly certain that the three young gunsels were not above murdering on a whim, capable of killing his brother just to see if the sights were set proper on the rifle.

But there was no proof. No fact. No truths. Only an itch down the spine, and a crawly feeling in his chest. Couldn't hardly go kill four men just because you had an itch you couldn't scratch.

A draft of sweet spices flirted with his nose, a smell of home filled his mind, and he thought of Ma rolling out the butter dough on her big board, then lifting the sheet on her rolling pin into a pie pan. Filling it up with apples and sugar, nutmeg and cinnamon, then topping it with the other sheet of dough, crimping the edges between her strong thumb and first two fingers with a certain loving gentleness. Then, like an artist, cutting little scallops over the top with her paring knife to look like a leafy fern.

Oh, that was a pleasure to watch when he'd been just a little tyke sitting on a high stool watching her bake, and her giving him the bowl to lick after the pies were in the oven.

Dreaming about home with Ma in the warm kitchen on a cold Sunday morning, he wondered how he could ever find such a small and precious thing again.

Strange how a man could try to make a whole life to fit around such a short, rich piece of childhood. . . .

Then he swallowed and realized he was salivating over just a dream and mentally kicked himself. While he was doing that, his eyes dropped to the steaming thick wedge of apple pie with the top browned and sugared, and little fern leaves carved in the crust.

=== 9 ===

SAM FIDGETED AT HIS DESK, MOVING PAPERS HERE AND there, wasting time. Skofer, looking a little better with some color in his face and more strength in his voice, sat in the extra chair by the door.

"Seems like you've got the bodacious fantods, Captain," Skofer said hoarsely. "Maybe you need a drink."

"I got somethin' for sure, but I can't put a name on it right now. If it was a longhorn bull tearing up my insides, I'd throw him, cut and mark him, and then slap my Flying B on his butt, and let him go off and sull awhile, but this critter inside me is ridin' me down."

Their strange conversation was broken up by the sound of a horse charging down Main Street at full gallop, then being hauled back and sliding to a halt before the marshal's office.

Bursting through the door came a short, wiry puncher wearing scarred bullhide chaps and a stained and battered Stetson. His face was weathered to a dried-out hide of grooves and wrinkles, browned to the color of beef roasted over a campfire.

"Come on, Marshal," he gritted, "we need you."

"Who?" Sam asked, getting to his feet, reaching for the Winchester .44-40 hanging on the wall.

"Chip Evans. Block Diamond. We were just gettin' moved in across the river. He's dead, I reckon, goddammit!"

"How?" Sam asked, moving toward the door.

"Rustlers. We just brought in six hundred stockers. Prime. Hardly had them settled on our range than somebody stole 'em."

"Skofe, mind the office."

Sam let the puncher take the lead. He knew where he was going.

Sam had heard of the Block Diamond moving in, finally talking the land office into honoring the papers, and he'd seen Chip Evans around town buying supplies, an older cattleman who obviously knew his business, doing just what Sam wanted to do himself. Starting out small, going at it a step at a time, building his house, a barn, and corral, finding his boundaries and learning the ground until he felt ready to bring in his first cattle and commence ranching.

He'd come up from Texas same as Sam and Skofer and Buddy, and he'd done what he'd meant to do, but now he'd lost it all. Hardly seemed fair.

The puncher led Sam to a ford over the river and drove his already sweating horse on south over an indistinct trail until they came to a sheltered flat where a primitive ranchstead had been established. The log cabin was obviously meant to be added to and finished later on.

"It ain't much," the puncher said, "but he had a notion he could whip it."

"I understand," Sam said. "When did they hit you?"

"Yesterday afternoon," the puncher said, leading Sam to the log cabin and on inside. "You can call me Shorty."

On the plank table Chip Evans had been laid on a

blanket, his eyes closed, his corpse rigid, the cup-sized chest wound caked with blackened blood.

"I wanted you to see how it was," Shorty said.

"He was shot in the back. Tell me."

"Me and Sorry Gallagher was here draggin' in logs from the timber to add on to the cabin. Chip had a wife waitin' over at Cooke City, and he wanted her here."

"The cattle?" Sam prompted the older cowboy, who had too many things on his mind to sort them all out.

"Chip was off on his bay, goin' through them, lookin' for grubs or fever, or anything—you know."

"Sure." Sam nodded.

"We heard the shots and here comes a gang of 'em, I don't know how many. Seemed like a hundred, I'll tell you. Anyways, me and Sorry run for the cabin, and whilst a couple of 'em pinned us down, the rest run off our horses, then they went back and just took the herd, the whole damned herd, and pushed 'em on upriver."

"That was yesterday?"

"Took me half the day and most of the night to find my horse," Shorty said, as if ashamed of himself for failing in his profession.

"And Chip Evans?"

"He was lyin' out there where they left him. Sorry and me brought him in here first thing this mornin'."

"Where's Sorry?"

"He lit out."

"Wanted for somethin'?"

"It ain't none of my business. He's a good enough cowhand. I mean, he ain't no gunslingin' rustler or nothin'." Shorty frowned.

"Price on his head?"

"Maybe. But I rode with him the past three years, and he don't even cuss."

"Let's go." Sam headed for the open door.

"Where we goin'?"

"I want to know what happened to those beeves."

"Not me," the puncher said. "Chip's dead, the cattle are gone, the ranch is wiped out, and I'm out of a job. I'm not about to chase after that gang for nothin'."

Sam could understand some of it. Shorty was loyal to his boss, the herd, and the ranch, and he'd risk his life defending them even though he was paid less than a living wage, but once the boss was dead, the herd gone, the ranch defunct, he would think about taking care of himself.

"So long, Shorty."

"That it?" Shorty asked belligerently.

"Not quite. When you've finished buryin' your boss, you can ride."

Sam mounted up and rode the red horse across the open country to the bed-grounds upriver half a mile.

The ruin of the Block Diamond ranch hit him harder than it might normally have done because the ranch was a model for his own dream place.

Oh, he'd rather have his cabin backed up against the north with the rimrock just behind, and maybe a better bottomland for winter hay, but this ranch wasn't too far off the mark. He could visualize himself working from dawn to dark, building up a home from nothing except bare land, and then have some rotten sonsabitches come and take it all away. Robbed of his ranch, robbed of his dream, and robbed of his life.

Red, always in a hurry, covered the ground quickly with his long stride, and Sam could see where the cattle had been bunched and driven upstream.

They had only a day's head start, and Red could maybe catch them in a few hours, but the rustlers seemed to operate with a precise plan, like a military maneuver, and any good commander would leave a rearguard, likely a couple of snipers ready to cut down on the first puncher that tried trailin' 'em very far.

The better part of valor was to outthink them and

make them go according to his own plan, not him to theirs.

There was no other way to go except northeasterly upriver. The Ogallala Range would cut them off from heading south until it petered out on past Bohannon's Bench.

It could be they'd cross the river and maybe try to take the beeves north, but the only market up there were Sioux, and nobody was crazy enough to try that.

So they would just drive them upriver to another hidden valley, change the brands maybe, look for a cut south, or try drivin' 'em on east into Dakota country, or hold 'em.

Either way, he could go back across the river and maybe come up on their flank and dog 'em on until he knew they'd stop awhile, then go back and try to raise a posse big enough to handle that many riders.

Thinking on that, he had his doubts as to whether there were that many brave and honest men in Elk City.

Say it was Saturday night and the town was overrun with punchers lookin' for excitement, likely he could get them movin' in the right direction, but it was three days to Saturday, and by then those beeves would be gone.

As he reasoned out the problem and worked out his own strategy, he rode across the ford, turned right, and made his way upstream, keeping in close to the trees as the river made its meandering turns and oxbows.

Sooner or later they'd come to the gap that led into Bohannon's Bench. There was no other way.

Likely they'd found a way out somewhere on the other side.

Thinking through this idea, he saw how someone had figured out how to use Bohannon's Bench, not only as a robbers' roost, but as a way of stopping any pursuit while the outlaws and their booty could take their time coming out on the backside and simply disappear in any direction they chose.

They were so arrogant, they hadn't even looked for old man Bohannon and bought the spread. They'd just taken it.

For damned sure, Bohannon couldn't come back to it, nor could he even sell it until the gang departed, feet first or otherwise.

Picking at the idea further, he wondered if someone had thought of using the plunder gained from the use of Bohannon's Bench to buy up the rights of neighboring tracts of land. Such a scheme would have no end to it.

Sam, you're actin' like a hound dog sniffin' a porkypine's butt, he told himself.

Being alert for a bushwhacker and taking pains to keep close to cover slowed him down considerably, but he was nearly sure of his destination, and saw no reason to take any chances that wouldn't produce some results.

He wondered who all was in the bunch that had roosted in Bohannon's Bench. It had to be run by someone with at least payroll money, imagination, and no conscience, a completely ruthless hombre with the cunning of a wolverine and the deliberation of a spider.

Maybe that was one positive thing he could do. Maybe he could learn who they were and call for outside law officers to help. If he didn't get bushwhacked on the way, he had a chance.

Kicking Red up to a fast gallop, he let the sorrel have his head over the open ground, covering three miles in something less than ten minutes. He figured the herd would travel not much more than six to eight miles a day, and by now he should be parallel with them. They were now, he estimated, three or four miles from the gap. After letting Red get his breath, he let him loose again, and the willing horse with the long stride soon brought him in sight of the gap itself.

Far off, to the right, Sam could hear the distant bawling of complaining cattle.

Looking up at the rimrock, he could see how the

sharpshooters could be placed almost anywhere so that they could shoot down into the open ground without much fear of returning fire.

Not far, back up north by the Absarokas, White Bear had made his fight and come up empty. What could Sam do against this forted-up bunch of lobos?

Securing Red in a patch of alders, he followed the stream to the point where the timber stopped and the rocky riverbed took over. The rustlers would have to come into sight in that empty space of desolation. They would have to go into the shallow water and walk the herd upstream through the gap, and then they could do whatever they wanted without fear of molestation.

Hunkered in the pile of driftwood logs that had mounded up against a boulder, Sam tried to spot the lookouts up on the rim.

They were well hidden, but he knew they were there. He knew if he stepped out into the open, they would kill him with their long rifles. He knew it, but he still couldn't see an extra shadow, or gleam of metal, or bird suddenly shying off.

No doubt about it, they were dead serious about their plan, whatever it was.

First the gold off the stage, killing two witnesses.

Next a herd of cattle, and the owner shot through the back.

The rattle of rocks and the bawling of the cattle came close, and then, almost near enough to spit on, a rider appeared and rode into the shallow water. Close by, the cattle breasted forward.

The rider wore Cheyenne leg chaps over ordinary Levi's, and a chambray shirt. The only thing unusual was the revolver tied low on his thigh.

As the rider turned to whip the leaders on into the water, Sam recognized Lonnie Sackbutt, the pasty-faced kid he'd had in jail just a few days before.

He wasn't much of a cowboy, because when he

whipped the leaders with his doubled lasso, the leaders didn't move any faster, and the following cattle backed up and tried to cut out through the timber.

Damn fool will run them beeves right over the top of me, Sam fretted, his .44-40 at the ready.

Lonnie Sackbutt passed on with the leaders, riding point, and went on through the gap.

The next rider on the flank had a face Sam didn't recognize, but he could see the sardonic cynicism on the stubbled features that seemed to announce, *Me first any way you like it.*

The left drag was Frank Arbole, sweating and whipping the cattle on, crowding them through the gap, as three riders on the yonder side were doing the same thing.

They'd been driving for almost two days straight, and they took their tiredness and anger out on the steers, even though it only made the herd harder to handle.

It took almost two hours to crowd the beef through the gap, and Sam was about ready to snake his way back to Red when he saw the last rider, the tall one, Mullins, with the quicksilver eyes and the hatchet face.

That made seven, and as the tall man was not really working the cattle, but rather seeing that nothing was left behind, Sam assumed he was the boss of the other six.

That would mean he'd been here earlier. It wasn't likely you'd send in the boss after everyone else. No, he would have been among the first. He'd looked over the hideout, made up his mind, then rode off downriver to recruit more hands.

It was this tall polecat who had led the way into the bank only three days ago.

Why?

Why had they gone into the bank and talked with Castor?

No wonder Castor had been so disturbed. They were forcing him into showing himself. They had done it right

94

then, right before his eyes. They'd made him their accomplice just by bringing Sam along to watch the unveiling.

No matter if anything could be proven in a court of law, Castor understood that Sam would know his involvement with these cutthroats.

Yet what would it gain Castor to have Buddy killed?

No, it still didn't make any sense. Buddy was no threat to anyone, and had never done anything to set a bushwhacker on his trail.

Coming to the gap, the tall one waited until the last of the drag passed on through, turned his horse in the shallows, looked carefully from left to right, as if trying to search out a spy, spurred his horse on through the gap, and then it was so quiet, a man might just ride out and take a deep breath of the good air for the pure pleasure of it, except if he knew there was a couple sharpshooters up there just aching to let the sweet air out of such a fool.

Next morning Sam broke his cold camp, and with a quick wash in the cold, sparkling river, set out on the trail back to town.

He knew he needed help if he was ever going to break into Bohannon's Bench, but he didn't know where to turn. He could wire the U.S. Marshal's office over in Virginia City, but the marshal over there was already doing the work of three and had no time to spare. It would take a hell of a lot more than two lawmen to break through the gap. He needed a troop of cavalry at least, and even that might not do it.

Those sharpshooters up in the rimrock had the latest Winchester repeaters, based on the ever-faithful Spencer, and to make a frontal assault against them, you'd need cannons.

There was a way into the bench from the back, but it was tricky because it backed up right into the Blackfoot reservation.

It was this back entrance that had spelled doom to

Bohannon because he couldn't guard both ends of the bench.

He'd said it was five or six miles back in the mountains, some little pass that would admit the hostiles.

He wondered how old Bohannon ever meant to put a ranch in there without a proper road to it. You could go through the gap if the river was low, but other times, you'd just have to set and wait for the spring flood to go down, and you could hardly run a ranch that way.

Framing the picture of the gap in his mind, he saw that to the upper side of it, the ledge was only a few feet thick, and eroded badly.

Put a couple boxes of powder in that fractured granite and you could blow out a wagon road in a day or two, he thought. Chances were Bohannon figured it out, but had to run before he could get settled.

Red was tired as they approached Elk City late in the day, but he was also hungry, remembering the oats in the livery barn, and Sam had a hard time holding him down.

"Fool horse." He smiled. "Don't you know it's bad manners to run to the barn?"

So it was that Red had his head high and his neck straining against the reins as they came down Main Street, ready to bolt to the barn at the slightest sign of Sam's permission.

Somehow the town seemed strange. Little kids were called in off the street. People seemed to fade into doorways, and no one said hello.

Stopping at the marshal's office, he dismounted, looped the reins over the saddle horn, and with a smile, slapped Red on the rump and said, "Go on, you don't need me."

At first Red couldn't quite believe it, but in a second he had it figured out and went on down the street toward the livery barn at an even trot, going fancy with his front hooves flicking a little extra, showing off.

Sam stood for a moment watching to make sure he

made the right turn, then sighed wearily, rubbed the stubble on his chin, and went on into the office.

"Skofe?" he called out in the dim light.

"Skofer's gone," came a familiar voice, "and you're under arrest."

In the gloom Sam made out the form of Elam Castor sitting at his desk. Off to the left stood a heavyset stranger wearing a badge and holding a long-barreled six-shooter pointed right at Sam's middle.

Off to the banker's left stood old man Zink, and next to him, Randolph Jack, a frozen smile on his larded features.

"Shuck that gun belt," the stranger with the badge barked.

"What the hell's goin' on?" Sam asked, alert.

"You're under arrest for the murder of Edward Starbuck," Castor said. "This is the new marshal, Clay Damkar."

"Mind!" Clay Damkar said, taking a step forward. "Right now!"

"Don't be hasty, Mr. Damkar," Sam said tightly. "I already heard of you, and I believe you're serious."

Sam unbuckled his gun belt with his left hand and let it fall, even as he was wondering where they'd managed to pick up such a notorious gunfighter on such short notice.

"Skofe?" he asked.

"The old bird skedaddled like a cut cat soon as he caught sight of Damkar." Randolph Jack chuckled, and Sam had the sudden thought that he'd like to stick a gun barrel up the lawyer's nose and tell him to laugh.

"Go on down the hall and pick any cell you like," Clay Damkar growled.

"Before we all get too carried away, why are you so sure I killed Starbuck?" Sam asked, knowing that once he was locked up, the chances of getting back out again were few and far between. "How was he killed?"

"As if you didn't know, he was shot in the back with a

.44-40 Winchester just like you carry. Everyone in town knows he was in the way of your romancing Miss Jean Louise. Ain't that right?" Castor said.

"That's right." Zink nodded. "I hear 'em talkin'."

"But I been thirty miles away from here for two days," Sam said.

"Can you prove it?" The banker grinned.

Suddenly it flashed through Sam's mind that Elam Castor knew everything. He knew Sam had crossed the river and found the rancher, Chip Evans, dead. He knew Shorty would drift on, and there would be no witnesses for Sam. He probably even knew that Sam had followed the stolen cattle clear to Bohannon's Bench.

As Sam looked at the four men facing him, he had the sinking feeling that they were all in it together, partners holding the trump cards that would put a rope around his neck, and the entire Elk River drainage would fall into their hands like an apple off a tree.

What could he do?

In Texas, Clay Damkar was known as a rustler and a border brawler who lived off what he could steal or sell his gun for. When the Texas Rangers had put a price on his head, he'd disappeared.

Sam had every reason to believe Damkar would shoot him down in cold blood if he so much as twitched his hands. It wouldn't make much difference to them how he was killed. It might look a little better to outsiders if they had a mock trial before they hung him.

"I didn't do it," Sam said easily. "I don't think you can prove I did it, either."

"Get in that cell." Clay Damkar kicked open the hall door and backed clear. "I don't need no proof of nothin' to blow your lights out."

Sam slowly advanced down the hall and entered the empty cell. Damkar slammed the door shut with a clang of iron and finality, turned the heavy key, and with a grin, said, "C'mon, boys, let's have a drink."

"I got to get back to the store," Zink said.

"I believe all of us have better things to do, Marshal," Elam Castor said in a thin voice that held a warning. "Maybe you better watch your drinking for a few days."

"Do what you want," Clay Damkar retorted. "I'll take care of my end."

"Bear in mind, Damkar, this man is a threat to all of us. If he should get free before we can hang him, he can do us considerable harm."

"What does he know?" Damkar growled back.

"I think he's made some good guesses," Elam Castor said with his thin-lipped smile.

"I wish you'd tell me what's goin' on," Sam said.

"Play dumb, cowboy, it's fine with me." Castor chuckled as if he had a bone caught in his throat.

Banker, lawyer, merchant, son of a bitch, Sam thought. They got you caught in a four-way hitch.

— 10 —

IN THE MORNING, SALLY MCKENZIE CAME INTO THE MAR-
shal's office bringing a tray with ham and eggs along with
toasted homemade bread, some wild plum jam, and half
a dozen hot cinnamon rolls.

Grudgingly, Clay Damkar let her in. He couldn't very
well prevent the feeding of his prisoner.

"When he's done you can bring me an order of the
same," Damkar told her.

"I can't spare that much time, Marshal," she said
politely, "but you're welcome to come on over and order
anything you like."

"Listen, girl." Damkar grabbed her free wrist. "I like
service, all kinds of service, understand me?" he said,
staring into her eyes. "Maybe you'd like me to search you
real good?"

"First things first," she said firmly, and carried the tray
down the hall and slipped it through a slot in the barred
door.

"Be careful, Sally," Sam said, taking the tray. "That
man is a purple-striped orangutan."

"I'll teach him a few monkey tricks I learned from the army." Sally grinned.

"Do you know what happened to Skofer?" Sam asked in a whisper, rattling his knife against the china plate.

"He's hid out with Doc."

"What are you two mumbling about?" Damkar yelled from the office.

"Billing and cooing, Marshal," Sally called back, and winked at Sam, adding in a whisper, "We're planning to get you out."

"Castor, Zink, Jack, they're all in it," Sam said. "You've got to be careful."

"That's enough," Damkar growled, coming down the hall, putting his hand on Sally's shoulder.

Whirling away from him, she snapped in a fury, "Get away from me, you big baboon! You stink worse 'n a squaw on a gut wagon!"

Damkar recoiled from her ferocity, then came back strongly. "I'll break you, lady, just as soon as I finish hangin' your friend."

"Maybe you'd better remember my dad is Colonel McKenzie, and his Fourth Cavalry regiment will be coming north right soon, cleaning out the hooligans on the way."

"I ain't worryin' about yellow legs," Damkar blustered, backing away from Sally.

He'd never worried about the future before, living day to day on what he could steal or extort, but now that he'd been promised a long-term position in the "company," his future seemed to have promise, yet no one had mentioned any colonel or Fourth Cavalry coming up from Fort Phil Kearny, and he suspected the banker of double-crossing him already.

"Just make sure your slate is clean," Sally said, "and maybe Dad won't hang you."

"There ain't nothin' against me anywhere," Clay Damkar said defensively.

"To tell the truth," Sally said seriously, "if I were in your boots, I'd just leave town before anybody did any checking."

"You're a long ways from bein' in my boots, miss." Damkar tried to play it both ways. He wanted to keep his tough bullyboy bluff going, but he wanted her to remember he spoke politely to her.

"I heard there was a price tag on your head in Texas," Sam said, as if trying to set the record straight. "I heard you used to dare those Texas po' boys to try and collect."

"That was just talk," Damkar blustered. "I got nothin' against me in Texas or anywhere else."

"Then I guess I can tell Daddy you're making sure your prisoner is getting fair treatment," Sally persisted.

"Of course. He eats better 'n me!" Damkar exclaimed, envisioning a thousand salty cavalry troopers coming up the river to keep the peace.

"I'm sure he'll appreciate that, Marshal," Sally replied seriously. Turning to Sam, she added, "I'll bring your dinner over later on."

"Yes'm," he said, trying not to smile.

She brushed by Damkar, taking Sam's clean platter along. Going down the hall to the office, she met big, white-bearded Cain King in his odorous buckskins, and she jumped a foot in sudden surprise.

"Steady there, little lady," King said in his rich, deep baritone, "I won't harm you."

"Sorry, Mr. King." Sally smiled. "You surprised me, that's all."

"Is the marshal about? I've got business."

"We got a new marshal; maybe he's temporary—"

"What do you want?" Clay Damkar came out of the hall and interrupted her.

King said nothing, but measured the man, his height, weight, color of skin and hair, and yes, any noticeable scars or blemishes, then, having had his look, said, "I got a bounty comin' for the product that's outside hanging over the back of my mule."

"You're the White Bear?" Damkar stammered, thoroughly rattled after Sally's news of the cavalry coming, and now the goddamned bloodthirsty bounty hunter who just might remember his face from a bounty bill.

"This was a good one. He's got two hundred dollars tagged on him. Strange how young he was and worth so much."

"Lemme look," Damkar growled, pushed by King, and went out into the street, where a few idle gawkers were gathering.

"Name is Shiny Freels," King said. "You can tell by his tin teeth."

While Damkar wouldn't admit it, he knew Shiny Freels without having to look at his metal teeth. After making a show of looking at the face, he said, "You shot him in the back."

"It's my way," the big man said calmly. "Took him at about five hundred yards. It's easier for both parties that way."

Going back into the office, Damkar searched through the desk until King said, "Can't read, can you? Well, this is the form, and we'll take it down to the bank and let Mr. Castor fill it out for us."

"You shouldn't shoot anybody in the back at five hundred yards," Damkar growled, standing up and going out the door after White Bear.

"Why not? Business is business." The white-bearded southern "gentleman" guffawed as he rolled along on his game leg toward the bank.

In the banker's office, Castor filled out the form and paid over the money after King signed it.

"Thank you, sir," King said, taking the money.

"Where'd you get him?" Castor asked casually.

"Upriver. They's a trail up that ways I figure I can

make a small fortune on." King grinned knowingly. "Outlaws thicker'n calf splatter up that ways just dyin' to help me along in my profession."

"Listen, King . . ." the banker said sternly, then didn't know what to say.

"You ain't goin' to tell me to let them polecats continue livin' and preyin' on innocent folks, are you, Mr. Castor?" The White Bear chuckled.

Castor wasn't sure if he was being gulled or not, but he knew he couldn't allow the big bounty hunter to pick off his men one by one.

"I'd just say be careful. You might make somebody mad at you," Castor said, his eyes flicking over to Damkar's face.

"I'll bear that in mind, but you got to figure a man has to make a livin'. Isn't that right?"

"I'm just saying it's dangerous. Maybe you'd do better and live longer if you drifted down into Wyoming."

"That's an idea. As soon as I sluice this bonanza upriver, maybe I'll do just that." King smiled. "Much obliged for your advice."

As soon as he'd gone out the door to deliver the body to the barber, Castor said to Damkar, "He's got to be stopped. Jesus Christ! Every one of those boys up there has a reward out for them."

"What about the Fourth Cavalry comin' up this way?" Damkar asked.

"You're crazy," the banker said shortly.

"Easy there, Mr. Banker," Clay Damkar growled.

"There's nothing to it," Castor replied more politely. "Where'd you get that idea?"

"The girl from the restaurant says her dad is Colonel McKenzie of the Fourth, and he's comin'."

"She's army all right," Castor muttered, "but I didn't know she was related to that McKenzie. Christ, he kicked the hell out of the Quehada Comanches."

"So what do you think?"

"We'll have to hurry it up, that's all. Don't forget, even McKenzie listens to congressmen, and we've got ours all wrapped up and paid for."

"But it ain't delivered yet."

Clay Damkar had the strange feeling that he ought to just leave quietly and then run like blazes.

"It's practically delivered. A million acres of the best grazing land in the country. We can't spook now!"

"Just so you know I ain't crazy, Mr. Banker," Damkar said softly. "When do we hang Benbow?"

"I'll get the court together and take care of it right away."

"It's got to look right. That McKenzie girl . . . she's watchin'."

"I thought he was sweet on the Starbuck girl."

"I don't know nothin' about it except the little filly has got some case on him."

"She could have an accident."

"Jesus God, you're a hard man!" Clay Damkar said, and went out the front door, leaving the banker to make his move.

Elam Castor was already thinking of how he could make some use of the Fourth Cavalry. Could he get a ruckus going with the Sioux and ask the cavalry to help move them on north, or the Blackfeet to the east? Could he sell them the cattle that were now having their brands changed up at Bohannon's Bench? Could he go in with Zink to sell hardware and dry goods to the troopers? Should he spruce up the Topaz and find some younger squaws to serve up to the love-starved troopers? There was money to be made when more than a thousand soldiers stopped by.

When Cain King left the bank with two hundred dollars in his poke, he knew exactly how he meant to spend it. Accordingly, he loped down the boardwalk with the peculiar sprung gait that seemed ludicrous to bystanders, but for those who'd ever suffered a broken bone, their second thought might be that it was probably extremely painful for him to walk at all.

Yet there was never a display of pain or joy on his pale face. In his eyes one could see little more than the haunted horror of a soul who has seen too many dead boys in blue and gray, stacked too high and too wide, billets of cordwood that could only make a mockery of a just and loving God.

King entered the mercantile and found the store nearly deserted. Zink shuffled forward through the gloom and said, "Good day, Mr. King. More ammunition?"

"No, sir." King walked over to the men's wear department and pawed through the ready-made suits hanging from a wooden bar. "I need a new outfit. A pair of black boots, stockings, underclothes, a black suit and white shirt with a dark blue four-in-hand cravat. I believe a low-crowned black Stetson should be sufficient."

"You're some big to fit—but there's one or two worsted suits there that might do it. You going to the city?"

"No, sir, I'm planning on going to the funeral."

"Miss Jean Louise's pa." Zink nodded almost reverently, took down the biggest dark suit in stock, and pressed the coat against King's shoulders. "That looks like it was made just for you," he said warmly.

Laden with his purchases, King went on down the boardwalk to Will Reese's Tonsorial Parlor.

Will Reese, a tall, thin, lugubrious man who served as barber and mortician, stared at the big man gimping into his shop, then put on his mournful smile, which you could take any number of ways, and said, "What'll you have, Mr. King?"

"First a haircut and a trimming of the beard down to a decent Vandyke, say, then a bath."

"Yes, sir. Have a seat and I'll make a real southern gentleman out of you."

"I doubt there's a barber in the world can do that," King said thoughtfully.

"In a manner of speaking, Mr. King." Will scrabbled to make his customer understand he was only a low servant desiring to please his master, who would give him a quarter for behaving like a dog.

"Get at it," King said shortly, the southern gentleness gone from his voice.

Later, after his bath when King was dressing, Will Reese gestured at the buckskin outfit tossed in the corner and asked, "You want me to dispose of these, Mr. King?"

"No. Keep 'em here. That's my business suit. Hard to find a squaw nowadays can make a new set like those."

"Yes sir." Will Reese folded up the buckskins and put them on a back shelf.

Looking in the mirror, King inspected his new appearance critically, stroked his white Vandyke beard, which matched the cut of his full head of hair.

Standing straight on his good leg, he appeared to be a wealthy businessman from the East.

"I wouldn't recognize you, Mr. King, if I wasn't in on the doing of it," Will Reese said noncommittally, neither sad nor glad.

"You'd know me by my goddamned leg," King growled back.

"Folks are used to that, Mr. King. It's nothing to worry about."

"No? I'd like to give it to you for a day or two and watch you climb the mountains and bring back the meat."

"Not me, Mr. King." Will Reese put his hand to his heart as a token of his obeisance, a gesture he thought

107

was becoming and good for business, but which was not at all genuine. "You bring them in and I'll plant them. Fair enough?"

"And the more the better, eh?" King smiled.

"You might say that, sir. Begging your pardon, Mr. King, but if you could figure a way to bring them in flat out instead of draped over a saddle, it'd make it a lot easier for me."

"What's the problem?"

"It's the rigor mortis, Mr. King," the barber said seriously. "I'm not complaining, you understand, but when I receive them doubled up like that, it's the very devil to get them so they'll lie flat in the box."

King's guffaw could be heard clear down to Milt Koberman's as he understood the barber's complaint.

"I don't get it. . . ." Will Reese looked puzzled.

"Change the box," King said, tired of the barber's servility, "or get an ax."

"You're foolin' me, ain't you, Mr. King?" Will Reese murmured.

King suddenly stood tall and assumed the stance of a challenged Jehovah. "I am the Lord of Sacrifice, the Master of Waste and Sorrow!" His voice reverberated with power. "I am the Destroyer, the King of Death!"

With that, King swung up the boardwalk, turned off on a cross path to Koberman's Livery, and hired the only buggy in town from the old man.

"Black horses, please. A smart, matched team."

"Yes, sir, Mr. King. I got 'em."

Once the team was harnessed to the buggy, King clambered up to the horsehide seat and drove the team a hundred yards down the weedy trail to Mrs. Riordan's Rooming House.

Tying the team to the gatepost, he set himself, touched his beard, and slowly knocked on the door with a massive fist, as if announcing the coming of doom.

Mrs. Riordan opened the door, her pinched red nose

poking out like a bloody dagger from under her sunbonnet, which she wore indoors or out, winter or summer.

"May I speak to Miss Starbuck, please," King inquired.

"Who is it? Oh, yes, I see now, Mr. King. Come in, Mr. King, and set down. She's finished dressing, I reckon."

He sat on the horsehide sofa, soft black hat in his hands, his back as straight as a rifle barrel.

When Jean Louise Starbuck entered the parlor, she gave the big man a look of consternation and wonder, expecting to see the giant slovenly bounty hunter in dirty buckskins.

"Mr. King . . ." she murmured.

He noticed first that she'd put her hair up in a tight bun at the back of her neck, making her face more heart-shaped, and that she was dressed in black serge, and carried a black hat with a heavy black veil.

"Miss Starbuck," he said, rising and taking her hand, "I came to express my condolences and to ask if you would permit me to accompany you to the service. I have a trap outside."

"How very kind of you. I thought I might have to walk for lack of any other conveyance."

King's heart was fairly bursting with pride and admiration for the young lady whose decorous manners were to his taste.

"I suppose we are late," she murmured.

"I'm sure they will not start without your presence."

He took her by the elbow and guided her to the door.

"Wait, please," she said, and quickly pinned the hat to her hair and dropped the veil down over her face.

Mrs. Riordan came out and patted the veil in place and said, "It's a sad day for you, my dear, but just remember your dear father's in heaven now, beyond all mortal care and woe."

King gallantly helped Miss Starbuck up into the buggy, then taking his own seat, clucked to the team, turning them on the tracks through the grass that would take them to a small knoll that had only recently been designated as the Vale of Tranquility Cemetery.

Up to this time there had only been a few outlaws that King had brought in and a sporting girl who had drunk a bottle of laudanum one cold night last March. She had been complaining about the constant scouring wind that sang strange songs to her.

Gathered at the graveside were Castor, Zink, Jack, Will Reese, a couple cronies from the Topaz, and the Reverend Everett Ellison. Close by was Will Reese's wagon with a plain pine coffin in the bed.

There was a buzzing of inquisitive voices as King helped Miss Starbuck to the ground and escorted her to the graveside.

After a few preliminaries and clearing of throats, the Reverend Ellison, a young, rosy-cheeked zealot with a yellow spade beard, in a thin, reedy voice, said all the nice things he could about the deceased, then opening his Bible to Psalm Twenty-three, commenced reading,

"The Lord is my shepherd, I shall not want . . ."

King closed his eyes to hide the unbidden tears that the long-forgotten psalm called up, and softly recited the words in unison with the preacher.

"He maketh me to lie down in green pastures . . ."

King's deep, resonant voice gradually gained in power as the Psalm brought his painful past to life again and swept him away.

"He leadeth me beside the still waters, He restoreth my soul . . ."

The preacher looked over at the giant man whose whole being was absorbed in the heavenly lyric, and let him carry on alone.

"Yea, though I walk through the valley of the shadow of Death,/I will fear no evil, for Thou are with me . . ./ Surely goodness and mercy shall follow me all the days of my life,/And I will dwell in the house of the Lord forever./Amen."

"Amen," the others responded.

Quickly four townspeople, using doubled-up lariats, lowered the coffin into the grave, and the young preacher stepped forward, picked up a clod of earth, and crumbled it into the grave.

"Ashes to ashes, and dust to dust."

Miss Starbuck commenced to weep, and seemed to sag toward the open grave, but King alertly caught her in his big arm and, steadying her for a moment, turned to the group, said, "We thank you for coming."

With that, his arm around her waist, he assisted her to the buggy and drove away.

The bystanders and onlookers stood in awe, as if they'd just witnessed a miracle.

As King stopped the buggy before Mrs. Riordan's house, Jean Louise Starbuck touched his arm and murmured, "I feel quite shaken."

"It's hard to lose one so close."

"More than that," she faltered. "May I ask how you managed to . . . ?"

"Recite the Psalm properly?" he finished for her. "I have not mentioned this to anyone, but it is proper that you should know that I was not only a colonel of infantry under General A. P. Hill, I was also named the regiment chaplain when we arrived at Antietam Creek."

"You were a minister to the Confederate troops?"

"I was raised to be a gentleman"—he nodded—"but of course, everyone on the plantation was educated in the gospel. As chaplains fell, I was given the extra assignment, and, my dear, before we left our dead at Antietam Creek, stacked like cordwood, for there was not room to walk otherwise, I said that Psalm so many times, I will be forever haunted by its music and its infidelity to the truth."

"Infidelity? It is in the Bible!" she protested.

"That day I saw thousands of young men, hardly more than country boys, wasted on the altar of God and slavery, and I tell you, when that long day was done, I cursed God for His easy words and false sentiments."

"That's . . . that's . . . blasphemy!"

"So be it," Cain King said heavily. "Man is naught but meat for Moloch, and whenever I can kill a man, I prove it one more time."

She looked into his eyes, wondering if the huge man was insane, but she saw only the mists of grief and betrayal.

"You must have faith," she said with compassion.

"No. Once I had faith in my home, my family, neighbors, the state of Mississippi, the United States of America, and, more than that, I knew there was a loving God who once said, 'Suffer the little children to come unto me.' But He said nothing about tearing our innocent youth to pieces and feeding them to the horror of Moloch."

"Surely . . . you can't be serious—"

"Miss Starbuck, I believe that God put me at Antietam in order to forge for Himself an avenging angel." King stared heavenward. "I am the Destroyer. I come from the Valley of the Shadow of Death."

"But—"

"There is no 'but,'" he said firmly. "You must accept me as I am, or we must part."

"Please come inside, Mr. King," she said softly, lifting her veil. "I believe we should not be too hasty."

— 11 —

Doc Newlin did not go to the funeral on the grounds that interments were contrary to his professional ethics.

He stayed close by his office, sometimes standing in the doorway observing the street's activities, sometimes drifting off to the back room, where Skofer, his arm freshly bandaged, waited and worried.

"Doc, I got to get Sam out of there," Skofer said for the tenth time that day.

"In due time," Doc answered patiently. "We need help."

"The whole town's against him. We can't wait much longer."

"There's where you're wrong. There's a number of decent folks here trying to make a home they can enjoy in peace and be proud of, too."

"They're not gunfighters," Skofer muttered, trying to think of some way to help Sam.

"Castor said he was going to have a jury trial. Some of our people will have to be on that jury."

"Banker Castor doesn't play fair, Doc. Even an old goat like me can see that."

"You're not an old goat, Skofe. You're a mature gentleman."

"I should have gone out and found Sam before he ever came back to town." Skofer frowned, his faded blue eyes worried.

"Nobody knew where he went. He could have been anywhere, and if they'd used you for bait, we'd all be in the pickle barrel."

Hearing a tapping at the front door, Doc shooed Skofer into the back room and opened the door a crack.

"Come in, Sally."

Carefully closing the door behind her, Sally looked around and said, "They're coming back from the funeral. Are you goin' to speak for us."

"I'll be there, but I'm not much of a spokesman. I thought Ira or Bert Stebbins, the blacksmith, would be better than I."

"No one wants to do it," she murmured, near to tears, her flashing dark eyes no longer merry and mischievous, and her bright smile faded into a firm, tight-lipped bar of determination.

"No one knows who to trust just yet. As soon as the dust clears a bit, we'll take a stand. Don't worry, Sal," the doctor said, hoping against hope that he was right.

He maintained his professional manners most times, keeping a grave countenance and an unhurried, measured pace, but deep down he wasn't nearly as confident as he tried to act.

"Listen to me, Doc," she came back strongly, "I may be just a silly girl most times, but I'm a born fighter, and I'll be damned if they're goin' to hang Sam without hanging me right alongside him."

"Now, now, calm down," Doc said. "He means that much to you?"

"Between you and me, Doc," she said firmly, "he's my man."

"Does he know it?" Doc tried not to smile.

"Not yet"—Sally made her own little smile—"but he will."

"Make sure every decent man and woman in town is out there in the square, Sally. Now, scoot." Doc was fearing that time was running out.

Going to the door, she paused, then pulled a .36 Colt six-shooter from her handbag and said, "I meant what I said, Doc. I'm not goin' to let 'em do it."

"Put that thing away," Doc said, vexed. "We'll handle it."

"That's more like what I wanted to hear." She went out the door.

Going to the back room, Doc looked in on Skofer and said, "I'm going to step out for a while. Stay right here so I won't have to worry about you, and I'll be back as soon as I can. All right?"

"Whatever you say, Doc, but I want to help."

"You'll be a real handicap if that bunch catches you, Skofer."

"Yes, sir," Skofer said, downcast.

As Doc came out on the boardwalk, he saw the people slowly collecting around the town square where someday they meant to build a courthouse and park and bandstand.

For now, though, it was only a level piece of ground with a plank platform where the fur trappers had traded with the Indians not so long ago. It was distinguished by a rare old ponderosa pine near the center, from which—nowadays, on the Fourth of July—old Ira Armsbury had a couple of muscular lads hang the Stars and Stripes all day.

Catty-cornered from the square was the jail and marshal's office, while in either direction the town straggled out to the grassland.

Women in their starched sunbonnets with children

hanging on to their hands or skylarking around slowly approached the square. Men drifted out of their shops and saloons in the same direction, although no signal or announcement of capital punishment had been made.

Elk City was so small that it needed no bell or town crier or bulletin board to bring the people out, and there were very few secrets among the inhabitants.

Odd to the doctor's eyes were the strangers all marked somehow with the same brand: low-slung revolvers, an untidyness about their person, a look of contempt on their faces, and eyes cold and hard as river stones. A tall one was sitting on his hipshot horse, apparently half asleep; another leaned against the front of the brick-walled bank; one occupied a bench across the street; and another lounged at the other end of the square. They were waiting, he realized; waiting for something to happen, and then they would follow instructions previously given them. They were part of a plan, a campaign already in motion.

Doc strolled on down to Ira's Café and found Ira stumping out the front door on his homemade crutch, his pain-lined face deadly serious. From the street came the burly Bert Stebbins, still wearing his leather apron. Joining them in a moment were Reverend Everett Ellison, Will Reese, and the bank teller, Boze Crowelly, who looked more nervous than usual.

Children were playing tag in the square, screaming and laughing, and the street dogs woke up and moved out of the way.

"What do you think?" Crowelly asked the group in general. "Is he guilty?"

"He's innocent until proven guilty," Doc said. "Isn't that right?"

"That may be right"—Boze made a jerky man-to-man grin—"but Mr. Castor thinks the other way."

"We don't owe your boss nothin', Crowelly." Bert

116

Stebbins glared at the slender teller, whose rubbery face twisted this way and that as a nervous tic developed under his left eye.

Doc wanted to get rid of Crowelly, who was probably a spy for Castor, but he wasn't sure enough to just tell the man to go on about his business.

Joining the group, Sally stared at Crowelly until he looked away. "What are you doin' here?"

"Now, Sally . . ." Doc said, trying to calm her down.

Ignoring him, she spoke hard and clear to Crowelly. "You get out of here. Go tell that coyote Castor that he isn't runnin' this town by a long shot!"

Crowelly glanced quickly around the group, seeking some support, but there was none. They all agreed with Sally but had been too timid to say so.

"You dumb clodhoppers, you might as well pack your bags—" Crowelly's voice broke before he could finish, and he retreated into a group of idle cowpunchers standing on the corner.

Sam Benbow heard the gathering crowd through his cell window and wondered if it was a lynch mob or a circus coming to town. While he preferred the latter, he realistically assumed it was the former, a small but noisy bunch of liquored-up vigilantes set on the warpath by one or all four of the ringleaders.

Of the four, Castor was the most powerful, but he needed the support of the other three. Each played an important role in the master plan, the least of them being the new marshal, Clay Damkar.

Yet Sam Benbow was determined that nobody was going to hang him until he had found Buddy's killer and seen that Skofer had a secure future. After that, he'd take his chances, but these were two debts he owed and he meant to pay them off.

At the moment he could see no way of escape. He had no weapon or implement to break him loose, but he thought if he could maneuver Clay Damkar into the right position, he had a chance.

Trouble was, Clay Damkar was no child in the tooth-and-toenail world of survival. He wouldn't come down the hallway for any reason although Sam had asked for a fresh jug of water and then a trip to the privy. Clay Damkar had said to wait, as if the wait wouldn't be long.

Sam walked restlessly back and forth in the cell and considered his moves if the bunch grabbed him. Somehow he had to find a six-gun. Two would be better.

For sure, if he could put a .44 up against Castor's bald head, there would be a cooling off of the bloodlust in the rest of them.

The door at the end of the hall was closed so that he couldn't hear what was going on in the marshal's office, but there was no way he could exploit his momentary privacy, and he decided that at the last possible moment he'd just cut his wolf loose, going crazy like a trapped animal, using teeth, boots, claws, anything he could do to hurt the men who meant to kill him.

While Sam paced the floor, and the townspeople waited for the marshal to bring out the prisoner, Skofer sat in the doctor's office, sneaking a drink of medicinal brandy and pondering a course of action.

He knew he wouldn't have a chance against Castor's crowd, but if he could just get around them somehow . . . Then he noticed Doc had left the bottom drawer of his desk half-open, and there, gathering dust, was a pearl-handled two-shot derringer next to a pair of bent forceps.

Skofer quickly checked the loads in the two-shooter, then opened the back door to the empty alley.

Standing unsteadily on a rain barrel, Skofer hoisted himself up on the shingle roof of the building and, hidden by the false front, clambered across until he reached the corner where the jail was situated.

Lying flat on the roof, he remained concealed enough

to hang his head down over the small back window. Despite digging his toes in the cedar shakes, he was slowly but surely sliding over the edge.

"Sam! Sam!" he whispered.

"I'm here," came Sam's voice. "Who's out there?"

"Me, Skofe, Sam. Catch!" Skofer croaked as he fell, tossing the derringer through the window at the last second.

In that movement, he twisted his body to make sure the pistol went through the window, but also insuring that his body would follow on around, and in a moment he was falling feet first to the alley.

Flexing his knees as he fell, he made a soft landing and let himself carry on the fall by hunkering down and taking more of the shock on his hands and wrists.

He'd never fallen off a roof before and wondered for a second why he hadn't broken his neck, but then, remembering drunks and babies always fell loosely, and aware that he was wanted almost as badly as Sam, he rose and made his way down the alley to the livery barn.

Best get ready, he thought, entering the barn. Old Milt, like everyone else, was up at the square waiting to see the exhibition, and Skofer had no trouble saddling up Red with Sam's saddle. Secured to the saddle was the carbine boot with the .44-40 still in it, fully loaded, and Skofer added an extra six-gun and cartridge belt.

After Red, he saddled his own buckskin and then wondered how he could get the whole jumble together, and him and Sam safely out of town.

He'd have to find a safe spot where he could be close to the doings.

In the front of the jail in the marshal's office, four men were divided in their last-minute plans.

"I say kill him right now!" Zink said. "That crowd out there is against us."

"No." Randolph Jack shook his head, and teased his fluffy sideburns with his index finger. "If the army comes in and finds out we've killed a prisoner in his cell, there'll be all hell to pay."

"I'll kill him out in the alley for a bonus," Clay Damkar growled, feeling in the pit of his stomach he'd waited too long to ride out of this town before it blew up.

"With the whole town waiting out there?" Castor asked, not expecting an answer. "We've gone too far now."

"There's another way," Zink said. "Suppose we give him an empty gun and he tries to escape. Clay can shoot him in front of everybody in self-defense, *Ja?*"

"That's a little better than just shooting him inside a locked cell"—Randolph Jack nodded—"but it needs a little dressing up."

"Like what?" Castor asked.

"Fake an accomplice, so it looks reasonable. The friend tries something with a rifle, a long shot. We never see who it is, only somebody blazing away at the old pine tree. Everyone starts running, Benbow gets ahold of a gun that's empty, of course, and it looks bad for everybody, including Clay here. Clay draws fast, and shoots in self-defense. The empty gun disappears. How's that for a story to tell the circuit judge?"

"Who uses the rifle?" Castor asked.

"Not me." Zink shrugged. "I can shoot nothing."

"How about that tall kid, Dicey Bohn? He can hit a flea's ass while he's jumping," Clay Damkar suggested.

"All right. I'll see that Benbow gets the empty gun." Castor nodded. "All them folks out there thinking they're so damned smart, they can stop the hanging, and by God, we'll just let 'em have their way." Castor made his thin-lipped grimace, and ejecting the cartridges from Sam's own revolver, which, with its holster and gun belt, was lying on the desk, added, "I think it is what you might call poetic justice. He'll go down with his own gun in his hand."

Sam barely had time to slip the two-shooter into his right boot before the door opened and Clay Damkar came down the hall with a six-gun in his right hand and the iron cell door key in the other.

"Time to go to trial." Damkar grinned, his eyes watching Sam, alert for any sudden move.

Unlocking the door, he stepped backward up the hall to the office and said, "Come along slow. I'm not goin' to put the manacles on you."

"Why not?" Sam asked with surprise.

"You're too good a man for those things." Clay's laugh sounded more like a dog coughing up grass.

Sam came slowly up the hall, aware already that something wasn't right. Any sensible person would hand-cuff the prisoner, especially one about to be hanged.

But they'd chosen not to. Why?

They wanted his hands free!

He'd recognized Skofer's voice, he'd seen his face as he fell off the roof, and he'd double-checked the cartridges in the derringer. There could be no false trickery in that small weapon, but there was something else on up ahead that they had planned for him.

At the doorway, Clay Damkar stepped back so that Sam had to pass in front of him, then, putting his six-gun in Sam's back, walked him out into the street.

"Head for that platform on the square," Damkar said.

Sam could see the women clustered together staring, kids playing, and off to one side Jean Louise Starbuck talking seriously and urgently to a white-bearded man in a dark suit, whom at the last second he recognized as Cain King. Then, grouped together at the corner, a larger group of townspeople gathered around old Doc, whose facial expression never changed.

Then Sam noticed the heavily armed idlers trying to appear half-asleep. They occupied the strategic corners, and were in position to cut down any man trying to escape from the square.

Castor's insurance, Sam thought, and recognized the tall one talking to Zink. He was nodding and then kicked his horse on down the street while at the same time hauling out a carbine from his saddle boot.

There were too many things to keep track of, Sam thought. They're runnin' a shell game not just on me, but anyone else that wants to play.

Half a dozen chairs occupied the platform, as well as a tall packing box that would serve as a judge's bench.

"Take the first chair," Clay Damkar said tightly, then added in a warm voice so unlike him, Sam nearly turned around to make sure it was Damkar speaking, "I'm sure hopin' they'll let you off."

"Thanks," Sam said, and sat down.

In the next chair sat old man Zink; next to him was Randolph Jack. Clay Damkar took the fourth chair, while, standing at the packing box, using Sam's old Peacemaker as a gavel, was Elam Castor, perky as a robin redbreast.

"Citizens of Elk City," Castor began as he pounded the box with the butt of Sam's gun, "come to order. Court's in session."

Looking over the townspeople, he saw the righteous determination on their faces that meant they would go against him and free Benbow if it ever came to a vote, and he was glad Zink had noticed the mood of the crowd before they'd made a big mistake.

Very well, they would soon eliminate Sam Benbow and that would wipe out any resistance the rest of them had left. After today the brave citizen who dared complain about the way things were being run would get a knock on his door in the night, and a bullet in the head when he opened it.

A million acres . . . a million acres . . . The phrase sang in his mind like a squeaking windmill, like a lark in the morning, like the clinking of gold pieces falling from a fountain. . . .

"All right, folks, we have a man accused of the cold-blooded murder of Edward Starbuck, and we're going to give you the evidence, and then we'll vote on hanging him. Mr. Randolph Jack will present the evidence."

Randolph Jack, glowing with self-importance, surreptitiously checked his fly, straightened his coat, touched his sideburns, and smiled genially at the crowd. "Ladies and gentlemen of Elk City, Professor Edward Starbuck, a well-known scholar and historian, was murdered two nights ago. He was shot in the back by a man lurking between the Topaz Saloon and Mrs. Riordan's Rooming House. You all know the lane. He was shot with a .44-40 rifle, and this is the bullet old Doc dug out of the victim. Isn't that right, Doc?"

"You're right so far," Doc answered in a clear voice, "but—"

"No 'buts' just now, please," Randolph Jack cut him off. "Now, we all know the accused owns such a rifle, but it has not been found."

Why didn't they look in my saddle boot where it always is? Sam wondered, and noticed that his six-gun, which Castor had been using as a gavel, was still lying unattended on the packing box, about a foot away from his left hand.

My Lord! he thought. They can't be that dumb.

He put his hand to his eyes as if bothered by a sunbeam or a mote of dust, looked closely at the Colt. With the butt toward him, it was hard to be sure if there was any brass in it or not, but at least he could see none. It was a shell game, all right. Give him an empty gun, then blow him to hell and gone.

That meant they were afraid of the vote, wanted to get

rid of him anyway. It meant they didn't give a damn about who killed old man Starbuck.

"So we know the accused had the weapon. Now, as to opportunity, where did you spend the night before last, Mr. Benbow?" Randolph asked with a flourish of his long, fine hair.

"I was upriver tryin' to catch up with Chip Evans's cattle."

"Anyone with you?"

"I was alone after Shorty left."

"And where is this man Shorty?"

"I guess he went downriver."

Randolph Jack turned to the audience, extended his arms, and opened his hands as if he'd just performed a miracle.

"There! You see, friends, he says he spent the night 'alone,' upriver, but he can present no proof of where he was."

"Get on with it," Castor said curtly, tired of the showmanship.

"Now, the motive. The most serious point of all." Turning to Sam Benbow again, he asked, "Have you known Miss Jean Louise Starbuck long?"

"About a month," Sam replied.

"Did she reject your advances?"

"I didn't—" Sam started to protest, but was overridden by the lawyer.

"Did she or did she not? Answer yes or no!"

"It wasn't—" Sam said.

"Yes or no!"

Sam clamped his jaw shut and refused to say anything at all, a surprise for the lawyer, who had thought he had Sam boxed in.

"Just a minute, please," came a female voice from the audience, and the crowd turned to see Jean Louise Starbuck pushing through.

A lane opened for her and she came up on the platform, her face pale. Still dressed in black, she showed a certain determination in her posture impossible to overlook.

"You have not been called as a witness," Randolph Jack said coldly.

"Let her talk, you coyote," old Milt Koberman yelled. The crowd came alive. "Let her talk! Give her a chance!"

Randolph Jack saw the banker nod stiffly, then casually elbow the six-gun a little closer toward Sam, and he noticed Clay Damkar ease his hand down to the butt of his six-gun.

"Please proceed, Miss Starbuck." Randolph Jack bowed gallantly.

"Sam Benbow never made any advances. He was only a friend I could talk to. My father, as you all know, had a weakness for the bottle, and I felt it my duty to tell Sam he was wasting his time on me because of Dad's problem. That's all there was. Sam often helped Dad home, which is a lot more than his drinking companions ever did."

With that she looked at Sam and said, "Sam, you're a good man, and everybody here knows it."

"That will be all, Miss Starbuck. Let me just say in rebuttal that I can call up half a dozen of those drinking companions of Edward Starbuck who will swear that Edward Starbuck forbade Sam Benbow from seeing his daughter again, and hard words were passed between them."

Castor, Zink, Jack, and Damkar waited for Dicey Bohn to let loose a volley from his rifle, and then finish off Benbow.

Sam was doing his own thinking. He could figure they meant to kill him right here on the platform and he could figure out how to avoid that, but he was worried about the gunsels spotted outside the crowd. If they got started shooting, there would be a quick and bloody massacre of innocent people, which had to be headed off before it got started.

That meant he had to get clear of the square, get clear of the whole town.

He could see that Clay Damkar was all set to shoot a duck in the rain barrel, and there would be no way to hold him back once the signal went off.

Standing and taking a step forward so there could be no suggestion that he had gone for the gun on the table, Sam said to Randolph Jack, "My turn."

"Sit down!" Randolph Jack snarled.

"I'm tellin' Clay that if he goes for that six-shooter, I'm goin' to put out his lights, that's all."

Sam sat down again, leaning forward so that his right hand was dangling near his boot top.

"What a showman you are, Mr. Benbow," Randolph Jack declared, trying to kill a few more minutes until Bohn commenced his diversion.

Raising his hand high as if making an oratorical gesture, he continued, "This scoundrel murdered an old man, helpless in drink, shot him dead center in the back at close range—"

Just then came the crack of the rifle from across the square.

"Watch out, Sam!" Jean Louise Starbuck cried out, seeing Clay Damkar bring up the Colt.

Throwing herself at the gunman, she grabbed at the revolver just as Clay pulled the trigger. At the same time, Sam palmed the derringer, pointed, and fired.

A bluish red hole appeared in Clay Damkar's forehead, and his pistol clattered to the decking.

Jean Louise Starbuck sagged slightly, then moved toward a chair.

"Oh, Sam," she murmured faintly, "I'm so sorry. . . ."

Sam couldn't hold back. Leaping sidewise, he caught

the banker by the shoulder and put the derringer against his pink, bald head.

"You're comin' with me!"

Shoving the banker ahead of him toward Main Street, Sam was hoping against hope that there'd be a couple good horses at the hitch rail.

"Tell your men, Castor—tell 'em even if I'm dead, I'm goin' to pull this trigger!"

"Don't do nothing, boys," Castor yelled, his face sickly pale. "Let him be. . . ."

— 12 —

KEEPING CASTOR CLOSE, SAM HURRIED TO THE STREET, BUT his heart sank as he saw only a couple small mustangs and an old mare at the hitch rail.

"Keep movin'!" Sam growled, pushing the banker on ahead of him, almost sure that a rifleman had a bead on his backbone.

"You're finished," the banker said, trying to get his breath. "The whole town is under my guns. I'll make you a deal—"

"You're goin' straight to hell from here," Sam said. "That's the deal."

Over his shoulder he saw Sally McKenzie running out of the crowd and following down the street.

"Get back, Sally!" Sam yelled, knowing that in a few moments the street would be full of flying lead.

Suddenly from the cross street, Skofer dashed out on his buckskin, leading Big Red, whose head was high and alert, muscles bunched and ready to explode.

Sally didn't falter in her pursuit; in fact, she had her bag open, and the small Colt appeared in her hand.

"Back, Sally!" Sam yelled desperately as he shoved the

banker facedown in the dirt and made a flying leap into the saddle.

Fast as he was, it wasn't fast enough. The rifleman had had Sam lined up all the way, just waiting for the banker to get clear, and all it would take would be the touch of a finger.

The banker slammed into the dirt, the finger touched, the bullet cracked free, and even as Sam hit the saddle, he felt the aching burn across his left side. The force of the bullet twisted Sam to the left and he lost the stirrup on that side as Red lunged forward, nearly out of control.

Sally stopped, kneeled quickly, used her left forearm as a rest, and aimed her .36 Colt at the man in the upstairs bank window steadying for another shot at Sam.

Crack! snapped the Colt. The man turned as if to aim the rifle at Sally, then lost strength as the bullet nicked his heart. Small as it was, it was big enough to drain the life out of him.

Staggering, the rifleman opened his mouth, but he was beyond screaming as his body pitched out the window.

"Where you goin', Sam?"

Sam didn't really know. All he knew was that he had to hurry.

"Block Diamond!" he yelled, and let Red loose.

The great, muscular animal leaped ahead, and with Skofer screeching out his Rebel yell close behind, the pair raced down the street, away from the town square, where Castor's riflemen had the townspeople covered.

The banker climbed to his feet, his face still pale, dusted off the dust of the street, and trotted back to the square.

Standing on the platform, he held up his arms and yelled, "No cause for panic, folks. You men with the rifles, you can git out of town. These folks don't need your help anymore!"

"Shall we go after him?" Mullins yelled from the edge of the crowd.

"Wait a minute, Mullins!" The banker motioned for Mullins to join him, and then said to Randolph Jack, "Tell these people to calm down and go on home; we'll see to it they're protected."

"What do you say, boss?" Mullins asked, coming close, his hatchet face hard and his eyes bleak.

"Bring the boys over to the bank; we've got to talk private," Castor said, and turned away.

As he hurried off to the bank, he was consumed by a mixture of rage that the plan had gone awry, and of a mortal fear for his life, now that he had personally come up against the power of the gun and felt the tube boring into his forehead, where the slightest movement would have splattered his brains out in the dirt.

The only way to cure that fear was to kill Sam Benbow.

He looked around for Sally McKenzie. If it hadn't been for her, Dicey would have blown Benbow out of the saddle with his second shot.

Before his train of thought could continue, he saw the blond kid with his head twisted strangely and his eyes blank lying on the steps before him.

Damnfool kid—teach him to make the first shot count.

Hurrying on into his back room, he washed his pink face in a basin of water, then returned to his desk and sat down in the big oak swivel chair.

Taking a deep breath and letting it out slowly in a long sigh, he felt the power coming back into him. In the street he'd acted like a yellow dog, but here in the quietude of his chambers, sitting on his throne, wielding the scepter of gold, he saw the million acres upriver in his mind, and once more became the Supreme Master.

The whole deal was nearly signed, sealed, and delivered. He'd brought in these tough shantytown kids who thought they knew so much, and with a little soft soap were willing to sign anything he put in front of them. If you could get a dozen fighting men like that, they could take up all the watered land in the whole drainage. A million acres practically in his hands by way of Randy's political connections, Zink's money and his own, and old Starbuck's stories in the newspapers back East.

Except Starbuck had proved out to be dead weight. His stories produced nothing to help pressure the politicians, and he'd turned into a talkative drunk.

Now, as he put his cold, analytical mind to it, all that was needed to bring the acreage into his hands was the elimination of Sam Benbow and—

That was it! Sally McKenzie! What had Benbow yelled to her as his horse was jumping around?

All he could remember was the thunder of hooves coming down close to his head as he'd made himself into a little ball, hunched over and hugging his legs to his chest. Horses plunging, rifles cracking, people screaming . . . What was it?

She'd yelled something first. . . .

What was it? *Where you goin', Sam?* That was it. He remembered trying to sort out the sounds in his mind as he'd expected to die. . . .

The horse had reared and whistled and whinnied. He remembered Sam's voice yelling, *Block Diamond.* . . .

That'd do it, he decided, beaming his reptilian smile. His plan came together automatically. He would kill two birds with one stone, as any general worth his salt should.

As the action moved down onto Main Street when Sam made his escape, Cain King rushed ferociously through the crowd to reach the platform, where Jean Louise Starbuck was surrounded by do-gooders and busybodies.

"Out!" he yelled, throwing people of both sexes aside. "Out of my way!" he roared, and fought his way into the inner circle, where Doc was kneeling by his beloved.

He saw the bloodred stain leaking through her shirt-waist. He saw the color leaving her face, and he knelt by her, his face close to hers, his eyes burning as she stared upward.

"I'm here, Miss Jean Louise," he whispered.

"What a pity," she said in the smallest of voices. "What a pity, Mr. King." A faint, sad smile touched her lips. "We could have made a life together. . . ."

"We'll do it. You and me, Jean Louise. We'll do it!" he groaned, seeing it all go away as he'd seen a thousand others go.

"Oh! Mary, Mother of God!" she whispered as the pain knifed into her body and convulsed in a drawn-out spasm, and death took her mercifully away.

The huge man bawled out, "No!" His eyes brimming with tears, hugging her close to his huge chest, he tried to force some of his own vigor into her, but there was no longer a response.

"I'm sorry, Mr. King," Doc said quietly, putting his hand on the big man's shoulder.

Easing the body of his beloved back to the platform, Cain King stood, and staring up into the heavens, raised both clenched fists and shook them at the sky, howling, "God damn you, God! How can you be so evil! How can you betray us! How can you be Moloch!"

Lowering his hands, he stared blindly at the crowd, tears leaking down his pale, flinty face. Suddenly he slipped into another universe of fire and pain, and screamed, "I am the Lord of Sacrifice! I am the King of Death!"

With that he plunged free and ran like a wounded bear, his right leg giving way under his powerful stride.

Sally McKenzie had been too confused in the action to realize at first that she'd just shot and killed a man. Things were happening too fast. Sam's big red horse plunging around, with Sam only half aboard, Skofer trying to grab the bridle while his own buckskin skittered about nervously, the rifleman twisting out the window and falling, the banker groveling in the dirt.

She heard Sam yell, *Block Diamond,* but had no idea what it meant. Of course, it was a ranch somewhere, but she was not acquainted with that particular brand. She was afraid to ask just anyone for fear they'd guess her reason for asking.

Shoving the small Colt back into her bag, she hurried over to the livery barn and found Milt Koberman just coming back from the square.

"I swear . . ." he said, shaking his head, "I swear I've seen everything now. Women gettin' killed, women shootin' men! I never thought I'd see the day!"

"Milt," Sally said with enough urgency to gain the old man's attention, "do you know the Block Diamond brand?"

"Hmmm . . ." he muttered, scratching his chin, thinking back, "I know that brand from somewhere. . . . Chip . . . Chip Evans was ramrod."

"Where is it?"

"What's left of it, I reckon, is across the river and up a ways."

"Thanks, Mr. Koberman." She went down the row to her own blue roan, waiting impatiently.

Quickly saddling him with her Mother Hubbard rimfire saddle, she led him outside and patted his neck a moment before swinging up in the saddle.

"Where you goin', girl?" Milt Koberman looked up at her, worried.

"I'm going to find Sam."

"I swear I've seen everything!" He bobbed his head and muttered to himself, "Women forking a saddle . . . shootin' . . . carryin' on . . ."

At Main Street, she meant to turn south toward the river, but coming directly at her were three riders, and she recognized them as Castor's hardcases. She wheeled the roan, only to see two more coming up behind her. They were young, tight-lipped, heavily armed, and with just enough insolence to show they were dangerous.

The exception was the tall, hatchet-faced rider with the killer's cold eyes, who was close to thirty and looked more like forty.

"Where you goin', ma'am?" he asked without touching his hat and nodding.

"I'm not going anywhere."

"That's nice." Mullins smiled thinly. "We're all goin' the same way."

They were already at the outskirts of town, and she was caught in the center of the bunch and was being pushed along down the south trail whether she wanted to go or not.

It was too late to yell for help, too late to draw her little Colt out of her bag, too late even to give a warning.

Sam let Red run full out for two miles in less than five minutes before pulling up to a slow lope.

After a time, Skofer's buckskin caught up with him, and Skofer called over, "How bad you hurt?"

"Some." Sam glanced over at the worried Skofer, then to make him feel better, said, "It's just a scratch."

"How come it's still bleedin' then?" Skofer asked doubtfully.

"'Cause I'm overblooded, Skofe." Sam didn't want to think about it just then. He knew he wouldn't be in the saddle if the slug had hit a gut or an artery. He could tend to the bleeding a little later. Right now it ached like hell and burned like a hot branding iron.

Have to put up with it. They had a lot of things to do, and the first was to get free of town. The second would be to find a camp where they could sort out the problems and go at fixing them one at a time.

"They ain't nothin' left of Block Diamond," Skofer said, "just the cabin."

"I know," Sam said. "I just didn't know what to tell Sally in a hurry, and I knew our best bet was to cross over the river that way."

They reached Chip Evans's failed dream before dark, and Sam rummaged through the cabin for whatever they could use. He loaded up a sack with a cooking pot, a canister half-full of cornmeal, and a whole smoked ham hanging from a rafter that Chip Evans might have been saving for a special dinner.

In one of the cupboards he found some clean, washed flour-sack dish towels. Stuffing them into his bag, he hurried on out to where Skofer was holding the horses.

"About now it's time we started bein' smarter 'n them," Sam said. "We'll make a clear trail back to the river, ride downstream, then come around through the timber to the head of the creek over yonder. . . ." Sam pointed to a small canyon across the flat.

"We can't make any mistakes, Sam," Skofer worried, holding back.

"That's for sure," Sam muttered, letting Red make a turn that could be easily seen. Anyone would know they'd come and gone again.

Reaching the river, Sam led the way downstream, through the shallow running water near the bank, until he came to a bench of decomposed granite, then turned back as he'd planned.

Clear of the timber, he could see the coulee across the small valley and made Red walk so as to make the smallest trail possible.

Before darktime they were safely camped in the coulee, the horses picketed on the grass.

"Climb that knoll, Skofer, see if you can see the cabin," Sam asked, stripping off his bloody shirt.

When Skofer reached the top of the knoll, he sighted through the gathering dusk and called back in a low voice, "Sure. There it is."

"Stay up there and watch," Sam replied, not wanting

Skofer to get nervous about the gouge across his ribs that had torn a furrow only a few inches from his heart.

After washing the wound in the cold creek water, he tore the flour sacks into strips and bandaged his midriff as best he could, hoping the bleeding would stop before morning.

He felt weak and dizzy as he finished, and he forced his mind to wake up and think. He knew they'd left a trail a mile wide leaving town, and hadn't tried to hide it later on. He knew Castor's gunsels would be coming along soon. He wished it would get dark. He didn't want to fight anymore this day.

He'd hoped to cook a little supper, but it was out of the question now. They couldn't risk the smell of smoke drifting across the valley.

"There's somebody over there," Skofer whispered loud enough to carry down to the creek. "A bunch of 'em."

"How many?"

"I make out at least six."

In a minute he'd clambered down the sidehill and joined Sam in the near darkness.

"Spread your blanket, Skofe. We're goin' to pass up supper," Sam said, lying down on his saddle blanket and fading away into a deep, healing sleep.

Mullins smiled to himself as they rode into the Block Diamond ranch, which had barely got started before he'd come along and cut the legs out from under it.

He'd taken Chip Evans down at four hundred yards, and as soon as the hands skedaddled, he'd supervised the taking of the cattle.

"Seems like home," he said to Sally as they rode into the ranch yard. She didn't answer.

"We'll make camp here," he called out to his people. "We can pick up his trail at daybreak."

"What about her?" came the voice of fat Ogden Santee from the gloom.

"She can sleep in the cabin," Mullins said.

"That ain't what I meant," Santee sneered.

"Don't get any ideas, Santee," the hatchet-faced gunman said. "She's goin' to be mine."

"How come?" Santee came back strongly.

In the darkness, Mullins had his .45 aimed at the vague shape of Santee. "You want to argue about it?"

"No, I'm just thinkin' it ain't fair."

"She's mine!" Mullins's voice cracked like a bullwhip. Then to ease off the tension, he added softly, "Maybe after I'm done with her, you all can have a go."

"That's more like it," Ogden Santee replied with a harsh laugh.

The others joined in with their approval.

"Get a fire goin'. Cook up some supper. Tomorrow we'll have Sam Benbow and his deputy for breakfast."

Sally McKenzie heard all of this and shivered with cold fear. Her hands were tied and she was helpless to defend herself, yet she had been raised to be a fighter, and she was in a frame of mind to fight with her teeth or anything else that might come to hand. If Mullins and Santee would just kill each other, so much the better.

Mullins lifted her out of the saddle, untied her hands, and pushed her into the cabin.

"You can eat later," he said.

"I'm not hungry and you can go to hell," she retorted, and quickly barred the door and felt her way to a rough bunk.

Alone in the darkness, she could let her fear show in the trembling of her hands and the worry in her eyes, but after a moment she got control of herself, slipped off her boots, and crept across the room to the cupboard.

Quietly she fingered through a cheesebox holding a few forks and spoons, but not finding what she wanted, ran her hands over the plank counter by the stove until her fingers found a slim boning knife with a six-inch blade.

Creeping back to the bunk, she slipped the knife into her right boot, then lay back with a sigh of relief. She had quit trembling.

As darkness settled over Elk City, Castor, Zink, and Randolph Jack were seated at a table in a corner of the Bonny Kate. Business was brisk, as the events of the day had unsettled the town's normal routine, but the three businessmen paid little attention to the comings and goings of the disturbed citizens.

As insurance, Castor had kept two of his young gunmen with him, letting Mullins take four with him to find Benbow.

That left the young pair, Lonnie Sackbutt and Frank Arbole, to guard Bohannon's Bench.

He'd lost Clay Damkar and Dicey Bohn, but they could be easily replaced in a few days. The main thing was to finish off Benbow, then wrap up the land before Colonel McKenzie came poking around.

"Can you handle McKenzie if he shows up unexpected?" Castor asked Randolph Jack.

"Those army people shine the boots of the politicians. Don't worry, one wrong word from me and he'll be breveted off to Gila Bend."

"I don't know. . . ." Zink shook his grizzled head. "There's too many people gettin' killed."

"It'll be over in a couple days, then you can mourn all you want," Castor said in a steely voice. "For now we give no quarter, and anyone wants to argue about it goes down."

"I told you it was a mistake to kill Starbuck," Zink argued. "All this started from that."

"He was worthless," Randolph Jack said. "Your share is bigger without him."

"And he complained too much," Castor said gently.

"Don't get any ideas." Zink rolled his eyes. "I got a right to my say. I got as much right as anybody."

"Don't talk so loud," Castor cautioned in a quiet voice. "Everything's going to be all right."

Zink, with his blocky features, with his fat melting downward into his dewlaps, stared into the pig eyes of the banker and saw the blackness of the abyss, the yawning chasm filled with black smoke, and said quickly but in a hushed tone, "Don't get me wrong, fellows, I'm in this to win. I don't talk and I don't complain. I just try to keep us sensible, *ja?*"

Glancing at Randolph Jack, he found nothing to read in the smooth, expressionless features, the fine sideburns —nothing.

"We're all partners," he protested, wishing he knew how to use a gun, "and we'll stick together. *Ja?*"

"Sure, Zink, of course." The banker nodded, wondering if he should be killed tonight or wait until everything was ready for the signing. "We're doing fine. Don't worry. Nobody's going to hurt you."

Zink knew in the back of his mind that he'd just heard his death sentence. The only thing he didn't know was when it was supposed to be carried out. But the front of his mind couldn't believe it. The front of his mind said that these men were friends as well as partners, and that they'd been through a lot together and would stay loyal to one another through thick and thin.

Suddenly the noise in the saloon quieted down as the batwing doors swung open and Cain King entered.

Dressed in his dirty buckskins, wearing a pair of six-guns and a bowie knife scabbarded in his gun belt, he advanced to the silent bar and said to Pat Duveen, "Whiskey."

Turning to look at each face in the bar, he saw the three conspirators at the far table.

"It's quite proper that there be a hush in this room," he said in his deep Mississippi drawl, "because the King of Death is here. The Avenger has arrived."

Castor's two bodyguards shifted their chairs slightly and let their hands hang close to their holstered revolvers.

Dismissing them with a contemptuous gesture, he raised the glass of clear whiskey and toasted the threesome in a clear, ringing voice, "To your soon and sudden death, goddamn your eyes!"

=== 13 ===

Sᴀᴍ ꜱᴛɪʀʀᴇᴅ ɪɴ ᴛʜᴇ ᴅᴀʀᴋɴᴇꜱꜱ. Tʜᴇ ɢᴀꜱʜ ɪɴ ʜɪꜱ ꜱɪᴅᴇ ʜᴀᴅ quit bleeding, but he felt worse than a calf with the slobbers. He winced as he sat up and watched Venus settling on the dark western sky.

But in this cool hush of early dawn, Sam felt an uprushing of his spirit. He felt as he had felt a hundred times before, that this was the way the world ought to be all the time, twenty-four hours a day. A world completely at peace, fresh, strong, clean, limitless, and full of hope for the coming day.

Slipping on his boots and hat, he touched Skofer's shoulder, then brought the horses in from the grass.

"Awake, Skofe?" he whispered.

"I'm tryin'."

"I want to move out before daybreak."

"We can do it."

Working by feel, they saddled the horses as a faint blush touched the eastern skyline. Sam swung aboard and set Red to walking up the long pasture close to the timber. Minute by minute the blush cast a stronger glow over the land, and before long Sam could see well enough to put Red into a slow trot, leaving the Block Diamond headquarters far behind.

"Perfect camp," Sam murmured to Skofer.

"You think they'll find it?"

"Sure, but it'll give us three, four hours head start. All we need, I reckon."

"Where away?"

"Bohannon's Bench."

"That makes sense. Instead of just lettin' 'em catch us, we just go into their camp and give ourselves up." Skofer chuckled.

"It won't be that way, old-timer." Sam smiled. "There was two killed in town. There's six back there at Block Diamond. I'm bettin' that leaves two to guard the gap."

"Well, hell!" Skofer exclaimed merrily, rolling his eyes. "One wounded Benbow is worth two back-shooters hid out in the rocks any day."

"Let's hope so. How's your shoulder?"

"Which one?" Skofer laughed. "My good one is twice as good as my bad one, so that makes me a hundred percent fit to fight!"

Sam shook his head at Skofer's ramblings. Couldn't cure him of it, didn't even want to.

Sam had ridden with many an old, soured puncher who'd suffered famine, flood, dust and drought, bugs and Indians, all for the sake of a rangy longhorn that he didn't even own, and then realized all of a sudden he was going to ride drag all the rest of his life. Them kind never said a word. They'd grunt high or grunt low, and you had to figure from there.

Compared to a saddle pard like that, Skofer was a real treasure.

By the time the sun was up, they were far upriver and the mountains were closing in on the drainage. Sam thought that they might have circled around, gone into

Elk City and had it out with Castor and his crew, but he reckoned that the gang's real power was centered in Bohannon's Bench, because it was there the stage's gold had gone, and there the stolen cattle had gone, and it was there that the owl-hooters had forted up.

If he could spoil their home base, he could face Castor on even terms at least.

Coming to a small creek, Sam rode into the timber and said, "We got to eat sometime."

"My stomach thinks my throat's cut." Skofer grinned and built a small fire while Sam mixed up the corn dodgers and sliced the ham.

He put the dodgers on a flat rock to bake near the fire, and put the ham he'd salvaged from Chip Evans's cabin in the pan. When the ham was done, he put the dodgers in the fat to fry.

It was a primitive meal, but it filled up the empty spaces, and Skofer pronounced it "Mighty fine belly-packin' material."

"Let's ride," Sam said after flooding the fire with creek water.

Sam moved into the timber on higher ground as they approached the gap, all the while studying the volcanic dike that had created the bench.

He knew at least two of the gunslingers who would be inside and probably on guard. One was the pasty-faced kid, Lonnie Sackbutt, and the other was his sidekick, Frank Arbole. There might be others, but those two had not been in Elk City the day before, so they had to be here.

Reckoning on human nature, Sam thought they'd likely stick together instead of spreading out on either side of the gap.

If there was a third loner who filled in the blank space, then Sam was going to look as foolish as a rained-on rooster.

For sure they held the high ground and could pot anybody trying to come at the gap straightaway.

The way the mountain hunched down on the north side looked like the place for a pair of lazy river rats to choose for a lookout post,

With any luck, then, the south side of the rimrock would be unguarded. Or, if there was a third man, and the luck was bad . . . Better to not think on it. A man did his best, and nobody could ask any more than that.

Mullins was in no big hurry. His main job was to either run Sam out of the country or kill him, and he figured it would be a lot easier for everyone if Sam Benbow lit a shuck for parts elsewhere. He had nothing to tie him to Elk City, not property nor family, not even a job. So why not just leave peaceable and start off someplace else.

Mullins saw no reason to press a fight if it wasn't necessary. Somebody always got hurt in a fight.

He reasoned that if he were Sam Benbow, he'd be riding off toward Wyoming or California by now.

When the sun was well up, he checked to see that Sally McKenzie was still safely locked in, and after a makeshift breakfast, they were all back on the trail.

They followed Sam and Skofer's long circle that doubled back to the river. He had to split the bunch there, sending a couple, Pawnee Dun and Bullard, upriver while Jess and Ogden Santee rode with him and the girl downriver, watching the bank for tracks.

The decomposed granite shelf that tilted up from the river revealed vague tracks, and Mullins sent Jess back to pick up the other two while he followed the trail with Sally and Ogden Santee.

They picked up the clear trail in soft ground, and about the time they reached the foothills and were turning upriver again, the other three of his crew caught up with him, their horses blowing and frothed with sweat.

"Foxy son of a bitch," Mullins said to Pawnee Dun.

"He's circling clear around to about where we were last night."

In the distance he could see the boxy log cabin and corrals of the Block Diamond, and shook his head with disgust.

"He watched us come in last night," he growled, and glared at Sally, who was considering when would be the best time to break loose.

They'd tied her hands in front so she could hold the reins, but they'd put a rope under her roan's belly and tied her feet to the stirrups, so that she had no way to get at the knife in her boot.

She could run for it and hope her roan was stronger and faster, but they had the guns, and if it came to a choice of letting her escape or killing her, she had no doubt which way they'd choose.

No, she decided, there had to be something to trigger off an action and divert their attention. She must be patient and wait for the right moment.

A little before noon they came to the coulee where Sam and Skofer had spent the night, and Mullins cursed as he saw the tracks head straight upriver. There'd been hardly a mile between them at daybreak.

They followed along across the pasture upriver until Mullins was fairly certain where Sam and his deputy were going.

"They're headin' for the gap," Pawnee Dun, the old renegade left over from the fur trade, said.

"I can see that." Mullins nodded. "Question is, should we go after him or go on back to town?"

"They can't get past Lonnie and Frank." Pawnee Dun bit off a chew of tobacco with his last two snaggleteeth, and waited for someone to tell him what to do.

"If he circles back to town, he can raise some hell, but if we spread out, we can block him and then squeeze him into the nutcracker," Mullins said, working out his plan out loud.

"Whatever you say," Pawnee Dun muttered, hoping they'd go back to town, where he could have a few drinks in the Topaz Saloon.

"Jess, you and Bullard cross over, and make sure he don't get by you. Fire off a couple of rounds if you see him, and we'll be right there."

The divided bunch followed on upstream. Mullins was fairly sure they'd have Benbow boxed in within a couple of hours. Now he had to think of the safest way of killin' both lawmen and endin' up with the girl.

"Don't be gettin' any ideas," Mullins said, riding close to Sally. "I'd hate to see you get caught in a cross fire."

"Why?" she asked plain out.

Her belligerence surprised him. Somehow he thought she'd soften up if he was patient with her, same as a colt is best broken slow and gentle.

"Because when this is over, I'm goin' to be ramrod of the whole shebang," the tall, hatchet-faced man said, "and I'll be wantin' to share my blanket."

"Not with me," she replied.

"You notice I ain't bothered you none yet."

"You're holding me prisoner."

"Lady, it could be some worse," he growled, and rode on ahead, then looking over his shoulder, he said softly, "and likely will be, lessen you quit shyin' on me."

From the timber, Sam could see the river flowing through the gap and the granite bastion on either side.

The pair of river rats should be stationed on the other side near the top.

"Skofe, you're goin' to have to be some nimble now, and I don't want you gettin' your head blowed off either," Sam said.

"I'm so nimble, I'm chain lightnin' strikin' a tree full of squirrels." Skofer grinned, his bony face set in mock concentration.

"Don't show yourself. Take my rifle and cross over.

146

Find a spot behind good shelter up near the north slope. A log or a rock, hear me? I don't want you takin' chances."

"I hear you, Captain."

"Once you're settled, take a shot toward the top of the rim, wait a minute whilst they get ready to pour the lead at you, then you fire off another so they'll know about where you are and turn up that way."

"You don't want me to sing 'Old Dog Tray' and do an Irish jig?"

"Damn it, Skofe, be serious," Sam growled. "Once they're pepperin' away at you, I'm goin' to snake in from this side and wade up through the gap."

"I can yodel real well, too." Skofer made his crooked grin and rolled his eyes.

Keeping well out of range, using whatever cover he could find, Skofer crossed the river and worked his way up close to the far foothills that lifted on up to craggy, snowcapped peaks.

Tying his buckskin in a thicket of lodgepole pines, Skofer sneaked forward with the .44-40 to the edge of the timber. He thought of running into the clear land and dropping into a deep buffalo wallow, which would give him good cover, but then he thought if he stayed in the timber, he could move about, and they wouldn't know for sure if it was one or two men shooting at them.

Might as well mix 'em up some, he thought. Using his good right arm, he levered a cartridge into the breech and laid the end of the barrel on a pine limb.

He had no idea of where the lookouts would be stationed, but he thought he'd take a crack at a slab of rock high up on the rim near the gap.

Sighting high, he touched the trigger.

When Sam heard the distant crack of the rifle, he studied the rocky bulwark ahead of him for some movement. If there was a third man on guard, he should show himself in some small way.

Nothing.

He waited for Skofer's second shot, and as he heard the two long rifles on the rim return the fire, he snaked forward through the grass. He was a dead man if they caught him out in the open like this, but he was depending on their attention being drawn in the opposite direction.

Skofer was firing, and from the reports of the .44-40, he was moving back and forth.

Good boy, Sam thought, coming to the bare, rocky shore, where he was fully exposed.

Sprinting across the gravel, he reached the river's edge where it poured through the gap.

Hip-deep in the swirling water, he held his gun belt and holster high and waded against the current.

A rifle ball splattered the water in his face, and he lunged forward, unable to do anything else.

Another shot came hot after the other, but this one was behind him. In another second he was in the gap and out of sight of the sharpshooters.

Striving to hurry, he took giant strides and found good gravel bottom as he went on and crossed to the other side.

He didn't bother to inspect the bench; better to concentrate on how to scale the rimrock.

Buckling the gun belt around his waist, Sam saw that on this side a jumble of large boulders made access to the upper rim possible.

The pair knew he was inside and behind them. They'd be coming back over in a moment, looking to pot him from above.

Somehow he had to draw them down or find a way to make the fight even.

Keeping low, scrambling with both hands ahead of him to keep from falling, he worked his way past their trail head, and went on.

Climbing upward through slim crevices in the rocks, moving from one side to the other, he tried to stay to the north. If he could reach their elevation, at least he'd have an even chance. Of course, they had the long rifles and six-guns as well, and there were two to his one, so it was never ever going to be a fair fight.

One of them was firing at random down into the rocks, trying to make him show himself, but the rifleman was too far south, and Sam climbed on upward.

Close to the top of the rim, he lay flat on his belly and caught his breath. When his arm was steady, he drew his Peacemaker and peered over through a cleft in the rock.

Frank Arbole was looking down over the edge, repeater rifle at the ready.

It was too long a shot for Sam's .44.

Squirming to the left, he felt the wound tear loose in his side and wanted to vomit from the sudden savage pain.

He touched his left hand to his side, and it came back wet.

Swallowing his spit, he rested a moment, then squirmed on another few yards. The rocky cliff was unstable; he could feel the small stuff shift under his boots, and he prayed the whole thing wouldn't slide out from underneath him.

Once again he sighted over a split boulder and saw Arbole hadn't changed position, and was firing at random down at the base of the dike.

Where was pasty-face?

He heard a rifle go off from the other side and realized Skofer was keeping Lonnie Sackbutt occupied.

Creeping forward again, he felt a rock give way under his weight and go clattering down the cliff. A moment later a heavy slug blasted the boulder in front of his face.

Arbole had him pinned down behind the boulder. He couldn't move one way or the other, but he couldn't wait, because Lonnie Sackbutt was just on the other side, and they'd have him in a cross fire if Arbole had sense enough to yell for help.

Sailing his hat over the boulder, Sam dived to the right and landed on his belly, with his Peacemaker ready.

Arbole was already bringing the rifle down from his angle on the hat to Sam's prone body when Sam squeezed the trigger.

Arbole's slug threw rock splinters into Sam's face, but Sam's shot took the sniper midway through the chest, driving him backward.

The rifle fell from his outstretched arms, his eyes looked at heaven, and he plunged over backward, down into the tangle of unyielding boulders. He didn't cry out. The sudden shock of the heavy slug kicked a grunt out of his voice box, and then he was gone.

Clambering on up to the rim itself, Sam saw the pasty-faced kid aiming off toward the trees, intent on picking off Skofer, who— The damned fool! Sam thought when he saw Skofer run out into the open, bend over, pat his butt, and run back into the trees. Sackbutt pulled the trigger and kicked up dust just where Skofer had been a moment before.

Next time he would be ready and lead him and kill him.

"You!" Sam yelled. "Hold it right there!"

Lonnie Sackbutt pretended he hadn't heard, and levering in another shell, seemed to be sighting off into the woods again when Sam yelled, "Throw it down!"

Suddenly the pasty-faced kid swung around and pulled the trigger even as Sam shot him in the throat.

Flopping back into his rocky nest, Sackbutt was dead as he ever would be. Sam holstered his six-gun, stepped forward, and waved his hat at Skofer.

He felt sick to his stomach, and the wound in his side was a sizzling red-hot poker.

Best you get down from here whilst you can, he told himself.

From his elevation he could see the broad, grassy bench and the river meandering through. The herd of cattle seemed too small to notice in the bigness of it all. On up near the river was a stone house with a shake roof, and on beyond was a close rim of high mountains.

Back in there somewhere, there was a pass that the Indians used, and through which Elam Castor had meant to send out the gold and the cattle and whatever plunder he took from the unwary to build his dominion.

By the time he reached the bottom of the boulder-strewn trail, he was weak and trembling from the pain in his side and the ooze of blood.

Leaning against a slab of granite, he rested a minute and then thought—what's the hurry?

"Carcass, you got to get to goin'," Sam said out loud. "They's a batch of rannies touchy as rattlesnakes in a skillet goin' to be here right soon."

Hearing the clatter of hooves on rock, he put his hand to the .44 and waited until he saw Skofer riding his buckskin and leading Red in from the gap.

"All over?" Skofer asked.

"I reckon." Sam nodded. "Quieted down some."

"Seems like you sprung a leak there under your arm."

"Fetch me out another flour sack, Skofe. We got to fix that blamed thing."

Skofer bandaged the wound, binding it as tightly as he could until Sam said, "That'll do."

It felt better being tied up tight like that, and the ooze of blood had stopped.

A bunch of cattle drifted by, and Sam studied their brands, puzzled for a moment, then he smiled. "Look how they doctored the brand!"

"Sure enough!" Skofer exclaimed, tracing patterns in the air with his finger. "They took the Block Diamond"

—he traced ◇◇ —"put ears on it, and made it into"

— ◇◇ —"a cut-glass sugar bowl!"

"Ten to one Sugar Bowl is registered in Elam Castor's name."

"That's enough evidence right there to hang him."

"We don't need any more evidence, trooper," Sam said. "All we need is the rope around his neck."

"We goin' back on top?" Skofer asked.

"Go on up ahead." Sam nodded. "I'll be there when I git there."

Slowly following Skofer up the trail, Sam found it a good deal easier than the way he'd gone up the other time. When he reached the top, he felt better. His bellyache had faded away, and his side seemed to be numbing down.

"They'll be comin' along pretty soon," Sam said, taking the long rifle that lay alongside the body of Lonnie Sackbutt. "Drag him off somewhere."

Glancing around, Sam saw cartons of ammunition, a box of dried jerky, another box of hard biscuit, and a couple of canteens poked into the rocky crevices.

When Skofer returned, Sam looked out over the barren approach to the gap and said tiredly, "Main thing is, don't let 'em get inside. Hurt 'em all we can and weaken 'em down. Then we see what happens."

"Be nice if the cavalry arrived. I just crave to see them cavalry men ridin' in with their flags a-flyin' and lookin' so fierce."

"Keep on dreamin' that way and we'll both be dead as fried mules," Sam said gloomily.

"How will they come?" Skofer asked, loading the magazine of the Winchester.

"I figure both sides of the river. Your job is to keep the south side clear, I'll take the north."

"It'd be better then if I was on down across the river."

"There isn't time." Sam shook his head. "Just find yourself a cranny that'll make a good fire lane, and make sure nothin' gets across it."

"I crave them crannies!" Skofer hooted. "Give me a little cranny, Fannie!"

Sam shook his head with a small, forgiving smile on his battered features and checked the rifle.

The .45 Springfield had buckhorn sights, and with a 405-grain slug backed by 70 grains of powder, it could kill a man at eight hundred yards, near half a mile.

Sam was ready.

=== 14 ===

MULLINS HEARD THE DISTANT GUNFIRE ON UPRIVER, AND when it quit he could figure that Benbow was dead or Lonnie and Frank were dead.

It hardly seemed possible that anyone could get at his lookout sharpshooters, and yet he didn't like the sound of it.

"What do you make of it, Pawnee?"

"I'm too old to hear good, but it sounded like at the end of each round, two guns went off at the same time."

"And what would that mean?"

"It would mean they were at close quarters. That means either our boys come down from the rim, or the others went up there."

"They couldn't," Mullins said.

"I ain't bettin'."

"We've got the girl," Mullins said softly as an afterthought.

"That'd bring 'em out if anything would." Pawnee nodded wisely.

"There's better cover on the other side," Mullins said, and led the way across a shallow ford and made for the timber. "Jess and Bullard will be comin' along," he added, trying to figure a new plan.

"Unless they got the fantods and went the other way," Ogden Santee sneered, and patted Sally's thigh.

"Damn you!" Sally snapped.

Mullins looked around to see Santee grinning at him.

"I told you . . ." Mullins glared at the lardy Santee with pure hatred.

"She's just tryin' to start trouble," Santee said, smiling insolently.

"Don't get nothin' started." Old Pawnee spit over his horse's ears. "We got company."

Mullins looked up and saw Jess and Bullard coming through the trees.

"What are we waitin' for?" Jess called out. "They ain't over on this side."

"Not on the other either," Mullins said. "They might have slipped through the gap, or we missed them along the way."

"Well, hell, there ain't nothin' to do around here but whittle toothpicks," Bullard grumbled. "You said down in Juárez, we'd see some excitement and make some money."

A small gnome of a man, Bullard was always nervous. His fingernails were bitten down to bloody rinds, and he constantly gigged his horse, then jerked him up.

"You want some excitement and some money, I'll give you a hundred dollars in gold if you ride on into the bench and find out what's happened."

"What's the catch?"

"We don't know but what the lawmen have the look-out," Mullins said.

"And nobody wants to venture out in the open and find out." Bullard grinned, and unconsciously gigged the bay, then jerked the reins and yelled, "Whoa! Goddamn you!"

"You'd make the hardest target to hit," Pawnee Dun said judiciously.

"Make it two hundred and I'll go in and clean out the whole snake's nest." Bullard glared at Mullins.

"Go in fast and hard and do your damnedest." Mullins nodded.

Not hesitating, Bullard spurred the rangy bay and then hung on to the saddle horn for dear life as the bay leaped forward. Getting his balance back as the bay raced out of the timber, Bullard leaned forward over the horse's outstretched neck and raced for the gap, lashing his quirt on either side.

He reckoned Lonnie and Frank would recognize the bay for his horse and favor him by holding their fire, but if Benbow and Haavik were holed up there on the rim, then he'd better lay a little to the offside with as much of his body hidden as possible and still stay on the horse.

Sam watched the bay and the small rider come tearing out of the timber into the open and murmured, "They want to test the water."

Calmly lining up the buckhorn sights on the small figure that—fast as his horse could run—was still in too much open space to make long-range speed important, Sam said, "I'll do it."

"I could, you know," Skofer protested.

"Sure you could, Skofe, but this one is tricky. I don't want to hurt the horse."

Sam let the rider come about halfway, making adjustments in his mind for the downward angle, and then said, "Dang it, I can't."

"Can't what?"

"Can't just shoot a man down at long range even if he's a polecat snake."

"Bark him, then, otherwise we're goin' to have to spend all day chasin' him." Skofer laughed.

"Maybe you're makin' some sense."

Again Sam lined up the diminutive rider, who was

standing in the stirrups and leaning far forward, screened behind the horse's neck, his butt poked up high, bobbing up and down.

Satisfied, Sam slowly squeezed the trigger without taking his eye off that bounding butt in the striped pants.

The report of the big Springfield in the lookout was tremendous and filled the space with powder smoke, but Sam had a moment's vision of the small rider spinning out of the saddle, and the rangy bay running in panic.

As soon as the smoke cleared, he saw the rider crawling back for the trees, one hand gripping his buttocks.

"Burned him right across his seater." Sam patted the rifle to thank it for being true.

He watched as a lanky gunfighter ran out to help the crawling man to shelter.

"Now they know."

"Know what?"

"Katie barred the door and they can't come home." Sam smiled.

"Why don't they just go back to town then?" Skofer asked, shaking his head for no reason at all.

"Because the stage gold is down there someplace, and the cattle besides."

"And maybe they just ain't sociable."

"That's the size of it. Boss sends 'em out to cut us down, and they got to do it or turn tail like a yeller dog."

"Feels good holdin' the hammer for a change, don't it?" Skofer chuckled and patted his hands together happily.

Mullins gritted his teeth as he watched Jess drag Bullard back into the trees, with the seat of his pants ripped out and a little blood oozing from his chubby backsides.

"The rotten bastard!" Bullard cursed.

"He did you a favor," Mullins said. "He could have parted your hair sidewise just as well."

"How we goin' to get 'em out of there?" Pawnee Dun asked the critical question.

"There's a way. I noticed it last week when that damned bounty hunter was clamberin' up there on the mountainside," Mullins said, "but it's goin' to take somethin' to get their attention."

"You've got it all figured," Santee muttered.

"Put a noose over the girl's head and dally it to your saddle horn, and keep your hands to yourself," Mullins retorted bleakly.

Ogden Santee shrugged his round, sloping shoulders, untied his lass rope, and set the loop over Sally's head so that it lightly encircled her neck.

"Now then, little lady," Mullins said, "you ride out there with Santee behind you. You make sure they see you, and then you ride right back here."

"What if I don't?" Sally replied strongly.

"I reckon we can all go down by the river and have us a picnic." Mullins smiled crookedly. "When I'm done with you, Santee can have seconds."

She stared at the tall, impassive rider with the hard hatchet face, and thought if she could just get him alone, why not just use her knife?

"You and me?" she murmured, trying to put a warmth in her voice that she didn't feel.

"You ain't goin' to be alone with any one of us until maybe dark." He shook his head. "Then maybe we'll draw straws."

"You devil!" she exclaimed bitterly.

"Oh, we'll pay you, dearie," Santee crowed. "We'll make you rich if you can perform."

"I'd rather die than have you touch me," she said vehemently.

"Oh, I like the little savages." Pawnee Dun grinned.

"Take her blouse, Santee," Mullins said.

Santee stared at him dumbfounded.

158

"Damn it, Santee," Mullins snarled, rode close to Sally, leaned over, and with both hands, ripped the cotton blouse loose from her upper body, exposing her lithe torso and firm breasts tipped with pink budding nipples.

As she futilely tried to cover her nakedness, Mullins gave his commands harshly. "Take her out there and show her around, then bring her back. I'll ride up the coulee and climb up to that far snag. When you see me up there, take her out again so I can get around the knoll, then bring her back in. By that time I'll have killed them. Understood?" His voice cracked like a repeating rifle, and the four gunmen, including Ogden Santee, nodded, cowed and obedient.

Wheeling his horse, he galloped off toward the northern slope, aiming particularly for a sheltering ravine.

Riding hard, he drove the horse as high up the ravine as he could go, then turned him back on a narrow game trail, letting him pick his way until Mullins judged he had reached an elevation higher than the rimrock.

From his position he could see his people far down in the trees, and he waved his hat for them to bring out the girl. Then, carrying his long rifle, he moved to a crag that extended from the mountainside like an ax head.

Crossing that exposed crag would put him in line of fire from the rimrock, but a little ways beyond, he would be in an excellent pot-shooting position and invisible to his quarry.

He waited until he saw the bare-breasted girl come riding out of the timber into the open, followed by Santee with the lass rope secured to his saddle horn.

Without hesitation, he stepped across onto the crag, and using an eroded crack to set his feet in, made it safely around the bulky stone block and found a bit of brush to hide behind.

Now he could see down into the rimrock lookout,

where Sam and Skofer were staring at the half-naked girl being exhibited just for their benefit.

Using a slab of rock as a rest, Mullins carefully sighted in Sam's head, then thought it better to make a more sure shot through the body.

Lowering his sights, he held his breath as he commenced squeezing the soft trigger when a heavy .45 caliber slug came howling out from nowhere and blew the top of his head off.

He never knew it. He would spend eternity sighting down the long barrel, holding his breath, squeezing the trigger.

Pitching forward, his body catapulted from the snag into the abyss of forever.

Sam saw it the instant it happened, but not before.

"Good Lord," Sam murmured, staring at the body pitching through space, the long rifle clattering down the rocks.

"Pretty near had us." Skofer shook his head. "We got us a friend someplace."

Sam looked down across the valley toward the river and saw a faint motion in the trees, then scraps of impressions through the flickering aspen leaves as the rider mounted and rode downriver—white hair, a pale horse, a white mule.

"The White Bear . . ." he murmured, still not believing all that he'd seen in the past sixty seconds.

Sally, the sniper, then Cain King!

"C'mon, trooper, they got Sally," Sam said, hurrying down the trail toward the bench.

Sally heard the rifleshot and saw Mullins dropping through space, and said a silent little prayer of thanks to whoever had sent that bullet so far and so true, and then she felt the rope tighten around her neck and heard Santee yell, "Back into the trees, pronto!"

She turned the roan with her knees and galloped back

into the timber with Santee close beside her, coiling the lass rope as he came close.

"Killed Mullins!" he yelled at the dumbfounded Pawnee Dun, Bullard, and Jess.

"Then they'll be chargin' out here in a couple a minutes," Pawnee Dun said, hauling his Winchester out of its boot and kneeling behind a fallen pine tree. "She's mighty strong bait."

Bullard was lying on his side whimpering, and Jess was looking at his horse as if he would like to make a run for it.

"They can't get down from there in any two minutes." Santee grinned. "I got time, all the time I need."

Taking out his sheath knife, Santee cut the bindings on Sally's legs and wrists, and hauled her out of the saddle.

"Get movin'," he growled, shoving her ahead of him until she stumbled and fell down a slope into a little grassy draw where a tiny stream meandered off to the river.

Landing on her back, she lost her breath for a moment, and Santee took that moment to dive on top of her, his heavy body crushing her down into the grass, his hand over her mouth, his other hand tearing at the buttons on her jeans.

Wild-eyed, she tried to bite him, but he cupped his hand tightly, then clouted her on the jaw. She saw the bleached skull come into her mind and tried to scream, then she saw the ghastly skeleton, the arm crooked, the hand extended, the bony finger beckoning.

Santee's fingers fumbled with the buttons as she blindly lifted her leg and found the handle of the boning knife with her right hand.

Ogden Santee was beyond sense, beyond reason, as he tore at her underclothing in brute lust.

Instinctively, her mind lost in terror, with all the strength in her right arm, she made the short arc and drove the slim blade into his larded back. She felt it scrape bone and then slide on deep into his body, clear to the hickory haft.

He arched backward in immediate reaction to the first pain, then his eyes widened in amazement and horror as a voice deep inside him told his brain that his lung had been pierced and a lobe of his heart had been opened, and his chest was filling with blood.

Sally jerked herself free as Santee pitched forward, blood retching from his open mouth.

He had not uttered a single sound. He had looked into space in terror without even seeing the bony finger beckoning to him.

"They're comin'!" Pawnee Dun yelled. "Get on over here, Santee!"

Coming to the edge of the draw, Pawnee Dun looked down and saw Santee's body shuddering in death's convulsions, and Sally on her knees rising, the knife in her hand.

"Don't bother, lady," he said quickly, "I'm leavin'."

Catching up his mustang, he mounted and yelled at Bullard and Jess, "You can hold 'em, boys!" then spurred the mustang off downriver.

"I ain't holdin' nobody," Jess said, mounting up.

"Wait for me!" Bullard cried out, and climbed gingerly aboard Santee's horse.

When Sally crawled back to the level, she dumbly found her blouse, slipped it on, and tucked the tails into her jeans so that when Sam and Skofer came riding in full tilt, she was at least mostly covered.

Sam holstered his six-gun and leaped from the saddle.

"You all right, Miss Sally?" he asked, confused by the sudden turn of events.

He'd thought that surely they would shoot him or his horse in his heedless, headlong charge across the open flat, but not a shot had been fired. Instead of a pitched battle, he'd found a very pretty girl, disheveled and empty-eyed.

"Sho' now, it's been a shock to you," he said gently, trying to see some understanding in those large, dark eyes, but there was nothing.

She was seeing the chalky, bony finger beckoning to her, and nothing else. She was feeling the knife blade grate over the bone, then slip so easily in.

"We're here, Sally. It's goin' to be all right now," Sam said, touching her fine, dark hair. "You can relax now."

But she didn't respond. She stared at the beckoning horror and it paralyzed her mind, blocking out Sam, the woods, the air, the light, everything.

"No," she murmured slowly to the beckoning finger bones, "I'm not going. . . ."

"Sam!" Skofer called, and Sam turned to where Skofer was pointing down into the draw. He saw the fat carcass, the puddle of blood, the knife wound in the back, the signs of struggle, and then he understood.

Turning to Sally, he took the slim boning knife from her willing hand and looked into her empty eyes again.

"I'm not . . . I'm not going. . . ."

"I sure hate to do this, Miss Sally," Sam said grimly, and suddenly slapped her with his open right hand so hard, her head turned with the blow.

She blinked, she squinted, her forehead creased with anxiety. What was going on? Who had slapped her and why?

As her eyes lost their glaze, she saw big Sam Benbow standing over her, and she reacted by immediately swinging her own right hand and slapping him back.

Then she said in a tiny voice, "I'm sorry, Sam, I didn't mean to do that."

"It's nothin'," Sam said with a big, happy smile on his face stained with gun smoke. "I'm sure glad to have you back with us folks, though."

She looked at the knife and asked, "Did I kill him?"

"In self-defense." Sam nodded. "You got more grit than eggs rolled in sand, girl."

"Can we go back to town?" she asked simply, tears brimming from her eyes, not tears of sorrow, but tears of relief and exhaustion.

"Yes'm," Sam said. "I just want to do one thing first."

Mounted up, Sam led them directly to the river and found a grove of poplars that he could still see in his mind's eye.

"This'll be it," he said, climbing off the red horse and sighting back up yonder at the crag that overlooked the rimrock.

Fingering through the fallen leaves and duff, he found the tubular .45-120-550 shell casing. He brought out the other one from his breast pocket and compared the two.

They were identical even to the off-center dimple in the primer.

"What is it?" Sally asked.

"You might say it's family business," Sam murmured sadly.

— 15 —

Randolph Jack, GOING UP THE STEPS OF THE BANK, stopped suddenly, stared up the street, then took the steps two at a time and hurried inside. Noticing that Boze Crowelly was gone, he hurried to the front window and watched the three riders come down Main Street like battle-weary troops who have fought long and hard to take a ridge, and having won the battle, are making sure they aren't going to lose it again.

"My God, Elam! They're back!" Randolph Jack's voice had lost its suave assurance and cracked into a hoarse moan.

"What is it? For Christ's sake, man, what are you staring at?" Elam Castor scurried from his desk to the front window and looked down into the street.

"God damn it," Randolph Jack groaned.

"An old loony, a girl, and Sam Benbow. You'd think eight good gunfighters could handle them easy enough."

"We've got to get out of here." Jack tugged at his sideburns nervously, his little eyes shifting as he considered the ways and means of escape.

"We need two more days at least," Castor said. "The land transfer is almost set."

"We don't have two days," Jack said. "We don't have two hours. That man knows everything."

"I'm not convinced he's bulletproof," Castor muttered.

"I know I'm not." Jack shuddered as he saw the determination on Sam Benbow's lined face, the set jaw, the hard eyes.

"Get your guts up, man," Castor snarled. "We've got a million acres of virgin ground in our hands, and you don't want to fight for it?"

"I do my fighting in a courtroom," Randolph Jack said nervously.

"Think a minute before you run yelpin' out of town with your tail betwixt your wet legs. The girl is no problem. The only problem is one man. He's flesh and blood, and a two-bore ten-gauge greener loaded with double-ought buckshot will cut him in two like it would anyone else."

"You can't just chop him down like that now. The town's behind him and ready to string up anybody out of line."

"Not if it's a fair fight." The banker's eyes glowed, and the confident, thin-lipped gila monster smile returned.

"You'd better have an idea that's one hundred percent sure thing or I'm heading west."

"Go ahead. I can handle it by myself. For your share, I'll be glad to tidy up Elk City," the banker replied.

"No you don't. I can read your greedy little mind," Randolph Jack growled. "I want what's mine."

"The wonderful thing about a short shotgun," Castor said, "is that you don't have to waste time drawing it out of a holster. You just point it and pull the damned triggers."

"Where do we get these greeners?"

"It happens that after I finished with Mr. Zink's

business, I took a matched pair as sort of a trophy." The banker unlocked a closet and brought out the pair of English shotguns with tight-grain walnut stocks and polished locks, beautifully engraved.

"One barrel is loaded with a solid lead slug. The other contains buckshot," the banker said, handing one of the pair to Randolph Jack. "All you need do is pull the hammers back, point in the general direction of Sam Benbow, then touch the triggers and watch him disappear."

"It's not that simple." Jack shook his head.

"You're right." The banker nodded agreeably. "But it is definitely going to happen."

"They're watching us," Sally said softly, hardly moving her lips.

"Fine," Sam said. "You better go talk to Ira and his missus. They're probably worried."

"And get cleaned up," she said. "Where are you going?"

"I think we'll just stop in at the Bonny Kate for a beer," Sam said casually.

"You goin' to fight 'em in there?" she asked quickly.

"Steady on, lady. Get yourself washed and we'll come over to Ira's for a piece of your famous apple pie later on."

"You're trying to sweet-talk me, aren't you, Sam Benbow, whilst you mean to tangle with that pack of coyotes!"

"Hush, child." Sam smiled. "I meant what I said. We'll have a beer with Pat Duveen and catch up on the gossip. We might just go stop at the barber shop for a scrub, and then I promise we'll come over for a piece of pie."

"Sam Benbow!" she said hotly. "I'm holding you to your word! Now, don't you go shootin' with anyone unless I'm close by."

"How close is close, child?" Sam teased.

"Just so you get it straight, I'm not any child." She giggled, touching his big, scarred hand with her own for an instant, then turned off to the hitch rail in front of Ira's Café.

"She's sure pretty, Sam," Skofer said, nodding agreement with himself.

"Tough scrapper, too," Sam said.

"You sweet on her?" Skofer asked vagrantly, his head turning left and right, keeping track of the possible ambush sites.

"Me?" Sam acted surprised.

"I wasn't just talkin' to your horse." Skofer cackled.

"I never knew a woman didn't bring a gunnysack full of problems along with her," Sam said noncommittally.

"You didn't answer me, Sam." Skofer grinned and rolled his eyes. "You know you didn't, too."

"I guess that's some kind of an answer, ain't it?" Sam said, and turned off toward the hitch rail in front of the Bonny Kate Saloon.

A few local people were scattered up and down the bar trading gossip, but when Sam and Skofer entered through the batwing doors, the room became silent, and one by one they drank up, nodded at Sam without looking into his face, and left.

"I'm not helpin' business none." Sam smiled at Pat Duveen.

"They're all nervous now, especially after Max Zink was killed."

"How?"

"I dunno. They found him yesterday morning in the alley behind his store with a bullet through the back of his head."

"Kind of thinnin' 'em out one by one." Sam nodded.

Drawing two glasses of beer and putting them on the bar, Pat Duveen added, "They can't find anyone to be marshal. Office is vacant."

"They can keep it," Sam said. "I'm hankerin' to raise beef."

"Found your place?" Pat asked.

"Bohannon's Bench." Sam nodded.

Before Pat could ask any more questions, the doors opened and Randolph Jack entered. His face was pale and a thin sweat greased his forehead. He carried, cradled over his left arm, a short-barreled, ornately decorated shotgun.

"Afternoon, gents," Randolph Jack said in greeting. "Glad to see you're back safely."

"Why?" Sam asked, eyeing the lawyer as he angled left to the other end of the bar and laid the shotgun carefully on the polished mahogany.

"Why? We need a good lawman, of course," Jack replied, and said to Pat Duveen, "A Spanish brandy, please."

"If I was a lawman, I'd outlaw the carryin' of shotguns in town," Sam said, slowly turning his body to face Randolph Jack.

"That's my equalizer. Don't worry." Jack tried to smile. "It used to be a little man could pick up a six-gun and be even with the big man. Now it's come to the point where peaceable citizens have to carry a shotgun to be equal to the gunfighters."

"Skofer, would you mind goin' outside and standin' by the door?"

"Sam!" Skofer protested.

"A favor," Sam said tensely.

"All right, Captain." Skofer frowned, finished his beer, and went out the front door.

"What are you worried about?" The lawyer forced a big grin.

"Tell the truth, I'm so worried about your equalizer, I think I'll just bring mine out on the bar, too." Sam drew his Peacemaker and scratched behind his ear with the front sight, a little smile playing on his face. "You happen to know who owns the Sugar Bowl brand?"

"Why?"

"Do you?" Sam's voice came back a little harder.

"It happens to be one of the brands of the Elk River Cattle and Land Company," the lawyer said, wiping the sweat from his brow with a linen handkerchief.

"You in that company?"

"I'm vice president."

"Who's president?"

"It's no secret," the lawyer said affably. "Mr. Elam Castor is the chief executive officer."

"Figures," Sam said, and heard Skofer suddenly yell out from the street, "No, you don't—"

He heard a clubbing sound and Skofer's voice broke off.

Sam without any hesitation shot the lawyer just above his broad nose, then whirled to face the batwing doors, which were already slamming open, revealing Elam Castor crouched low, holding the butt of the second shotgun against his right elbow, ready to fire.

There was that fatal instant when to pull the triggers would win the battle, but in that single instant, Skofer, dropping from the blow to his head, managed to grab the banker's boot with his free right hand as he fell.

In that fatal instant, the banker's aim was turned slightly, and he had to correct it. In that fatal instant, Sam fired the big Colt directly at the gleaming shotgun itself.

His heavy slug caromed against the forestock, skidded along the walnut beavertail, smashing it into brittle splinters and driving on.

Castor dropped the shotgun, stumbled to his knees, clutching at his paunch with bloody hands.

With anguish the banker saw Randolph Jack crumpled to the floor, his shotgun still on the bar.

"You didn't give him a chance," the banker gritted out, staring up at Sam.

"He was a fool," Sam said harshly. "He went to the left, but he was right-handed. Took twice as long to turn and make his shot."

More than blood was staining the banker's clutching hands. He looked to see the greenish yellow muck dripping through his pink fingers.

"Get the doc," he groaned.

"Doc can't fix that kind of a gutshot," Sam said casually, reloading his Peacemaker.

"Get the doctor!" the banker screamed, weaving from side to side as the agony bit deeply into his belly.

"I wouldn't piss on you if you was on fire," Sam said, stepping around the slow-dying man whose howls were not much different from those of a gutshot coyote.

"You all right, Skofe?" Sam asked, helping his partner to his feet.

"Took a knock on the old *cabeza*," Skofer said, then added with a grin, "Maybe that'll do me some good."

"Knock or not, you'll do to ride the river with."

"What's that awful noise?"

"Banker's takin' his losses kind of hard," Sam said. "Let's go have the pie first and then a bath and then some more pie."

"And then a couple of drinks." Skofer smiled and pounded Sam on the back with his good right hand.

"It ain't that easy," the rich, cultured muddy-bottom voice called from down the street.

"We're goin' to have us a piece of pie, Mr. King. Why don't you come along?" Sam asked, getting ahead of Skofer and stepping out into the street. "I reckon I owe you somethin' for savin' my skin up at Bohannon's."

"I paid back what I owed you and made it even, except for . . ."

"Except for my brother Buddy?"

"No, sir! I mean to say except for your breaking the heart of my true love!" Cain King yelled, his southern identity lost in a red rage as he remembered Jean Louise Starbuck. "You stole her from me and then you broke her heart, and she still died to save your useless life!"

"My brother Buddy," Sam said flatly, "down by Yellow Creek a couple weeks back."

"I don't know nothing about your brother! But if I killed him, I'm damned glad of it."

The two were now facing each other in the street sixty yards apart and walking toward each other a slow step at a time, both touching their six-guns with their fingertips as they advanced.

"I'm sure sorry about Jean Louise," Sam replied. "She was too much of a lady to fit in my life, or yours either."

"You killed her. You broke her and killed her!" King roared, his eyes wild as a runaway bronco's.

"My brother Buddy . . ." Sam said levelly. "Why did you bushwhack him?"

"That fella in the blue frock coat? I recollect now. I killed him because he looked a lot like Red Handley."

"I'd almost forgive that, knowin' who you are, King, but why didn't you bury him?"

"He was meat!" King raged wildly. "I am the Lord of Sacrifice! I am the King of Death!"

With his hand on his six-gun, King became the Destroyer, a killing machine operating automatically and mindlessly.

Even as King was throwing out his challenge, Sam knew that the draw had to come at the end of his taunt as sure as the sun sets in the west, and was already drawing before the speech was ended.

Still the King of Death was faster and his bullet nicked Sam's left leg, knocking him down as he fired.

His bullet caught King in the left shoulder, spinning him around and driving him down to his knees. As King raised his revolver for another shot, Sam's second bullet punched him in the chest and knocked him backward into the dust and dried horse manure.

Crawling forward, Sam knelt beside the giant man who was still struggling to get up off his back.

His eyes stared into the cloudless sky and a serenity came over his bitter features, a gaunt smile touching his lips. "Ah . . ." He breathed shallowly.

A thin bubble of blood burst on his lips, and his voice returned to the soft, reverberating drawl of the Mississippi mud. "I thank you kindly, sir, for your favor. . . ." His gaze seemed to fix on some distant object as he continued. "Jean . . . ah, my dear Jeanie . . .

"The Lord is my Shepherd, I shall not want.
He maketh me to lie down in green pastures . . .
He leadeth me beside the still waters . . .
He . . . restoreth my soul. . . ."

=== 16 ===

Sam and Skofer left Doc's office shorn of bandages, and although their wounds were scabbed over cleanly, they still favored the sore spots.

"Now, don't get shot up anymore," Doc growled at them as they left. "I'm gettin' damned tired of workin' on the same carcasses all the time."

"What if I was to come down with flat feet or arthritis of the brain, something really hard to fix?" Skofer grinned.

"I'd give you a bottle of whiskey and tell you to go drink it." the Doc smiled.

"What'll we do now, Skofe," Sam asked, "whittle or play mumblety-peg?"

"Don't get in such a hurry." Skofer laughed. "Old Bohannon, he'll be here soon enough. It won't hurt you none to set in the Bonny Kate and watch awhile."

"I want to get up there and start fixin' up that stone house. Winter's comin'."

"He said he'd come on today's stage. Ain't that fast enough for you?" Skofer frowned.

Crossing over to Ira's Café, Sam said, "Coffee?"

"If that's all they got," Skofer said dryly, and they drifted into the café.

Hardly had they got their elbows on the counter than Sally was putting thick mugs of hot black coffee in front of them.

"Good morning, gentlemen," she greeted them cheerily. "What would you like?"

"This'll do," Sam said absentmindedly, thinking about the ranch and all that had to be done before winter.

He was thinking that old Bohannon had the right idea locating the stone house right near to a hot spring that ran year-around, winter or summer.

You could pipe that hot water right into the house once you capped it off.

If he could get a batch of copper pipe like they used in the steam engines, he could probably heat most of the house just using that spring.

Course, it would be nice having a fireplace, like they had down in Texas when he was growin' up.

He remembered how he'd come in wet from feeding the stock or dragging a cow out of the bogland, and hunch up against the fireplace while the steam rose right over his head, and Ma would say, "Sammy, now you get out of those wet clothes and get into somethin' dry. . . ."

But he'd hold off because the warmth coming through the seat of his pants felt so good, and he could hear Ma out in the kitchen mixing syrup with the dried apples and pokin' in some cinnamon and grating nutmeg, and him thinking how nice it was to come home to a warm fire with Ma cookin'. . . .

Then he felt the handle of a fork being put between his fingers, and looked down to see a thick wedge of hot apple pie looking back at him, and then he looked up and saw Sally smiling.

About the Author

Big Sur Writer

Writing Westerns

by Jim Cole

The Coast Weekly

JACK CURTIS JUST HAD TO WIND UP WRITING WESTERNS. ONE grandfather, his favorite, ran a saloon in a dusty cowboy town in western Kansas and had met Jesse James. Rumor had it he may have shot a man.

"Being an average boy," Curtis said, "I was enamored with this stuff a lot more than by my other grandfather—who was a straight, up-and-coming cattleman." Those extremes—the gunslinging ne'er-do-well and the honest owner of a thousand-acre ranch—produced Curtis.

Most of the year Curtis and his wife, LaVonn, can be found either at their Apple Pie Ranch in Big Sur, or in San Juan Bautista, where he works in a humble two-bedroom house, a photo of his mustachioed and steely-eyed grandfather ("my no-good grandfather," Curtis said) watching him. His career—through poetry, short stories, novels, and Hollywood—has gone full circle. Curtis has settled into his western writing. It's a genre that he never really escaped.

Like so many midwestern farmers, the Curtis family was driven from the land in the 1930s. "I'm a Dust

Bowler," he said in an interview in San Juan Bautista. "Not exactly the Joad family, but close enough. My father lost everything. I believe he stole the car we drove west in. Loaded it up and took off, and sold our stuff as we came over to buy gas."

In Fresno, his father left him and his mother. Curtis began working to help make ends meet, but he knew he wanted to write. He went to Fresno State University, where he edited the campus newspaper and began writing and selling poetry. After a military tour during World War II, he decided to abandon journalism, turning down a job offer at the *Fresno Bee*. "I thought I could affect the world in a positive way more as a fiction writer," he said. So he began to write in earnest, making a living by building houses while LaVonn taught school.

In the late 1940s he struck upon the idea of self-sufficiency, and he and LaVonn staked a claim in the Los Burros Mining District in Big Sur's Los Padres National Forest. "I wanted to see if I could live without taxi cabs," he said. Five miles from Highway 1 without utilities, the two planted orchards, raised chickens, and tried to live off the land.

"The thing is, we couldn't. We kept going broke," Curtis said. "I could never get the writing going to make much money at it. But I was a great idealist. I still am." So in the late fifties they moved to Prunedale to build a home and settle down. Christmas Eve 1960, just shy of completion, their home caught fire and was destroyed. But that wasn't all they lost. "My best novel was burned up in this fire, and I hadn't made copies," he said.

Director Sam Peckinpah, a high school friend, came to his rescue, offering him a job as a Hollywood scriptwriter. He caught on fast and soon was working on his own, selling his services to the highest bidder. For twelve years he worked for Hollywood writing for a batch of popular shows, including *Have Gun Will Travel*, *Wagon Train*,

The Rifleman, and *Zane Grey Theater.* In addition, he wrote for *Doctor Kildare, The Corrupters* and *Ben Casey.*

Jack and LaVonn built another place in Big Sur. Their Apple Pie Ranch has electricity and phone service, so he could work for Hollywood from there. But twelve years of Hollywood was plenty. "I was fifty years old and I was worn-out," he said. "I was tired. I was just finished with it."

Ten years later he was off on another adventure, building a house in Mexico. Every October he takes his typewriter and research books and moves to Baja California, where he can write from sunrise to sundown.

Six years ago an agent asked him if he had any westerns. His response was not surprising. "I'm a natural western writer."

With one and a half westerns, *The Sheriff Kill* and *Texas Rules,* already done, Curtis began examining what was on the market. He was not impressed. Gee whiz, he thought at the time, westerns are really going downhill, or I've changed.

And he told himself, I think there's an opportunity here for a good writer, in all modesty.

"I want to get the writing, I want to get the poetry, to get the humor, I want to get the music," he said. "I don't want to be one-dimensional. I want to be three-dimensional."

Curtis has become a stickler for accuracy, researching dates and historic events, studying guns and inventories from nineteenth-century general stores. Last year he and LaVonn returned to the Midwest and drove from Texas to Montana, following the trail of the last cattle drive as part of his research of his most ambition western, *Purple Iris.*

On a shelf in his San Juan Bautista study he has the *Book of Inventory of Beeman & Co.,* from an 1892 general store in San Francisco. He flipped through the pages and read about hairpins, Indian muslin, cocaine for eighty-four cents, Jamaica Ginger (used in bootleg whiskey), hay rakes, bridle bits, cartridges, and a revolver for $5.20.

On another shelf he has a replica of an 1860 army Colt .44 revolver made by his son. There is also a collection of books—the *University of Chicago Spanish Dictionary* beside the Bible, *Cowboy Slang, The Best of the American Cowboy,* and an *1897 The Century Atlas of the World* that shows western Nebraska empty, western South Dakota nothing.

And above the books is a century-old photo of a mustachioed fellow wearing a wide necktie and a jacket. He has the steely gaze of a man who could very well have shot somebody and will watch over his grandson trying to write about it a century later.

THE BEST WESTERN NOVELS
COME FROM POCKET BOOKS

H. B. Broome
- [ ] THE MAN WHO HAD ENEMIES..............66186-8/$2.95

Sam Brown
- [ ] THE LONG SEASON........67186-3/$3.50
- [ ] THE CRIME OF COY BELL..............78543-5/$3.99

Robert J. Conley
- [ ] QUITTING TIME..............74364-3/$3.50
- [ ] STRANGE COMPANY..............69476-6/$2.95
- [ ] BORDER LINE..............74931-5/$3.50
- [ ] THE LONG TRAIL NORTH..............74930-7/$3.99
- [ ] NED CHRISTIE'S WAR....75969-8/$3.99

D.R. Bensen
THE TRACKER
- [ ] #1: MASK OF THE TRACKER..............738345-8/$3.50
- [ ] #2: FOOL'S GOLD..............73835-6/$3.50
- [ ] #3: DEATH IN THE HILLS..............73836-4/$3.50
- [ ] #4: THE RENEGADE......73837-2/$3.50
- [ ] #5: RAWHIDE MOON..............73838-0/$3.50
- [ ] #6: DEATHWIND..............73839-9/$3.50

Jack Curtis
- [ ] THE FIGHT FOR SAN BERNARDO..............79319-5/$3.50
- [ ] CUT AND BRANDED.....79321-7/$3.99
- [ ] WILD RIVER MASSACRE ....79320-9/$3.99

R.C. House
- [ ] TRACKDOWN AT IMMIGRANT LAKE........76042-4/$3.50
- [ ] REQUIEM FOR A RUSTLER..............76043-2/$3.99
- [ ] SPINDRIFT RIDGE..........76044-0/$3.99

Jim Miller
THE EX-RANGERS
- [ ] #1: RANGER'S REVENGE..............66946-X/$2.95
- [ ] #2: THE LONG ROPE......66947-8/$2.95
- [ ] #3: HELL WITH THE HIDE OFF..............73270-6/$3.50
- [ ] #4: TOO MANY DRIFTERS..............73271-4/$3.50
- [ ] #5: RANGERS REUNITED..............73272-2/$3.50
- [ ] #6: THE 600 MILE STRETCH..............74824-6/$3.50
- [ ] #7: STAGECOACH TO FORT DODGE..............74825-4/$3.50
- [ ] #8: SHOOTOUT IN SENDERO..............74826-2/$3.50
- [ ] #9: CARSTON'S LAW..............74827-0/$3.50
- [ ] #10: STRANGER FROM NOWHERE..............74828-9/$3.99
- [ ] #11: SOUTH OF THE BORDER..............74829-7/$3.99

Bruce H. Thorstad
- [ ] THE TIMES OF WICHITA ....70657-8/$3.50
- [ ] THE GENTS..............75904-3/$3.99
- [ ] PALO DURO..............75905-1/$3.99

Simon & Schuster Mail Order
200 Old Tappan Rd., Old Tappan, N.J. 07675
Please send me the books I have checked above. I am enclosing $_____ (please add $0.75 to cover the postage and handling for each order. Please add appropriate sales tax). Send check or money order–no cash or C.O.D.'s please. Allow up to six weeks for delivery. For purchase over $10.00 you may use VISA: card number, expiration date and customer signature must be included.

Name _____

Address _____

City _____ State/Zip _____

VISA Card # _____ Exp.Date _____

Signature _____

728-01

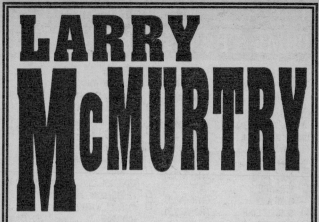

LARRY McMURTRY

*The Acclaimed Novel that Inspired the
Academy Award-winning Motion Picture*

Terms of
Endearment

and its stunning sequel...

The Evening
Star

*"In Aurora Greenway, Mr. McMurtry has created an
unsinkable character as memorable in many ways as
Scarlett O'Hara."* —Atlanta Journal-Constitution

POCKET
BOOKS

Available from Pocket Books

935

LARRY McMURTRY

The Pulitizer Prize-winning Masterpiece!

LONESOME DOVE

(Available in paperback from Pocket Books)

And the Spectacular Sequel...

STREETS OF LAREDO

(Available in hardcover from Simon & Schuster)

POCKET
BOOKS